$\underset{5}{}$ Reasons
You'll Lo...

D0625076

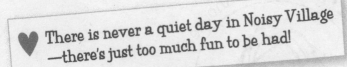

♥ There is never a quiet day in Noisy Village
—there's just too much fun to be had!

♥ Lisa and her friends are unforgettable
characters; they turn any playtime into
an exciting adventure.

♥ By the much-loved author of
Pippi Longstocking, Astrid Lindgren.

♥ Full of charming stories that capture the
freedom and imagination of childhood.

♥ Per... ...reading aloud at bedtime.

Meet the Children

Lisa · Middle Farmhouse

Lasse · Middle Farmhouse

Bosse · Middle Farmhouse

of **Noisy Village**

Anna • North Farmhouse

Britta • North Farmhouse

Olle • South Farmhouse

Kerstin • South Farmhouse

OXFORD
UNIVERSITY PRESS

Great Clarendon Street, Oxford OX2 6DP

Oxford University Press is a department of the University of Oxford.
It furthers the University's objective of excellence in research, scholarship,
and education by publishing worldwide. Oxford is a registered trademark of
Oxford University Press in the UK and in certain other countries

Text © Astrid Lindgren 1952, 2001 Saltkråkan AB
Illustrations © Tony Ross 2016

Translated from the Swedish by Susan Beard
English Translation © Susan Beard 2016

This translation of Nothing But Fun in Noisy Village originally published in Swedish
published by arrangement with Saltkråkan Förvaltning AB

The moral rights of the author, illustrator, and translator have been asserted

First published as Bara roglit i Bullerbyn by Rabén & Sjögrn Bokförlag in 1952
This translation first published in the UK by Oxford University Press 2016

Database right Oxford University Press (maker)

British Library Cataloguing in Publication Data
Data available

ISBN: 978-0-19-273946-9

1 3 5 7 9 10 8 6 4 2

Printed in Great Britain

Paper used in the production of this book is a natural,
recyclable product made from wood grown in sustainable forests.
The manufacturing process conforms to the environmental
regulations of the country of origin.

Nothing But Fun in
Noisy Village

Astrid Lindgren

Translated by Susan Beard · Illustrated by Tony Ross

OXFORD
UNIVERSITY PRESS

CONTENTS

NOTHING BUT FUN IN NOISY VILLAGE

My name is Lisa and I'm nine years old and I live in
Noisy Village. Mum says she thinks it's only called Noisy
Village because us Noisy Village children are so loud. You
wouldn't believe six children could make such a racket,
she says. It sounds as if there are three times as many of
us, at least. As for me, I think Lasse is the loudest. He
makes as much noise as ten normal boys, I know that.
And Bosse and Olle are not exactly quiet, either. Britta
and Anna and I are quiet at least some of the time.

Anyone who wants to come here to Noisy Village
has to go up lots of steep hills one after the other,

because Noisy Village is so high up. If it was only a *little* bit higher people would be able to pull the stars down from the sky with a garden rake, says Lasse. We've got such a lovely view from Noisy Village because we live so high up. Although of course it's almost only masses of forest you can see, but there are many people who think masses of forest is beautiful to look at. And they come here and look. Once a very grand lady arrived in a car, and she had a girl with her.

'We only wanted to see the view,' said the grand lady. She was wearing a red coat and a red hat and was so beautiful. Her daughter was also beautiful and she had on a light blue dress with a little red brooch. She was called Monika, the girl, and was about my age.

Mum said wouldn't they like to come into our garden and drink some cherry cordial. She told me I should talk to Monika. I would have liked Anna and Britta to be there to help me, but they had gone to Storby Village on an errand and weren't at home. Lasse and Bosse and Olle were at home, but they didn't talk to Monika. Oh no. They just stayed behind the corner of the house, being silly.

Sometimes they peered round and said something, and laughed loudly at what they had said.

'Are those your brothers?' asked Monika.

'Only Lasse and Bosse,' I said. 'Not Olle.'

'Which one is Olle?' asked Monika.

'He's the one with not much hair,' I said.

But at that moment Lasse came striding past on his stilts. It was only to show off, I'm sure. Lasse's stilts are so high that when he's standing on them he can look in through the windows of the first floor of our house. He did that once when I was up in my room playing with my dolls. All of a sudden I saw Lasse sticking his head through the window. He lifted his hat and said:

'Good day, madam, and how are you this fine afternoon?'

I was very scared at first but then I ran to the window and that's when I saw Lasse walking on his stilts. It was the first time he had tried them.

But now he was showing off for Monika. He strode around on his stilts in our garden and shouted to Bosse and Olle:

'You get a very good view from up here!'

Agda, who helps Mum, was about to go and feed the pigs. She had stood the bucket with the food leftovers outside the kitchen door. And of course, Lasse had to blunder about and fall off right there! He tipped everything out of the bucket and then landed right in the middle of the pig food.

'Now we've got a very good view too,' said Bosse, and laughed and slapped his knees. Monika laughed as well. Lasse took himself off to the outhouse and stood under a tap to get clean. Then he came back soaking wet but just as cocky as before. He wrung the water out of his hair, looked at Monika and said:

'The things you do to make people laugh!'

Mum had him go indoors and put on dry clothes, but he was quickly back out again. And then the boys also talked to Monika. Well, not Olle of course, because he just won't talk to people he doesn't know. But then all of a sudden he said to Monika:

'Do you want to see my little sister?'

And then he ran home to his house and fetched Kerstin. Kerstin is only one and a half. Olle loves her so much. And that's not surprising because Kerstin is so sweet and Olle doesn't have any other brothers or sisters. Olle put her on Monika's lap and Kerstin yanked Monika's hair so hard that a small handful came out. But still, that didn't make Monika cross. I expect she knew that little children always do that.

I stood looking at Monika's brooch. And then I said:

'What a lovely brooch you've got.'

'Do you want it?' asked Monika.

But I didn't—I mean, that wasn't why I said it was a lovely brooch.

But Monika took off the brooch and put it in my hand. And her mother said I should have it too. Even though *my* mother said:

'No, that won't do at all . . . !'

But I did get the brooch and it was full of small red jewels and it was the most beautiful brooch I had ever seen. It's mine now. I keep it in a box in my chest of drawers.

After a little while Britta and Anna came home from Storby Village, and when they caught sight of the car on the road their eyes popped wide open. Cars hardly ever come to Noisy Village because this is where the road ends, and anyhow it's so narrow and twisty. Britta and Anna stood by the gate and didn't dare come into our garden while Mum and Monika's mum were sitting there drinking cordial, and we were talking to Monika. But then I shouted at them:

'What are you standing there gawping at? Haven't you seen people before?'

Then they came in and said hello to Monika, and Monika said:

'How many children have you actually got in this village?'

'Six and a half,' said Lasse, because he thinks Kerstin is so little she can't be counted as a whole child. But then Olle got angry and said:

'You're a half yourself!'

We told Monika that Britta and Anna live in North Farmhouse and Lasse and Bosse and me in Middle Farmhouse and Olle and Kerstin in South Farmhouse.

'I'd like to live here too, I really would,' said Monika.

After Monika's mum had finished her drink she went and sat in the car and so Monika had to go as well, of course. Her mum looked at the view once more, and then she said:

'But isn't it terribly boring and humdrum living way out in the forest like this?'

Then Mum said:

'We have so much to do, we don't have time to think about it.'

I thought Monika's mum was a bit stupid saying what she said. It isn't boring or humdrum at all. I think we have nothing but fun in Noisy Village.

Then the car drove off and Monika waved at us until she disappeared from sight.

I don't think we'll see Monika any more. All that's left of her is the brooch. I let Britta and Anna have a little turn each at borrowing it.

Afterwards we ran up to Grandad who lives in one of the two attic rooms in North Farmhouse. He is Britta and Anna's grandad, and he is almost blind. But he so very much wants to know about everything that goes on in Noisy Village that we simply had to tell him about the car and Monika. Grandad says that if we weren't here he would never find out anything, because none of the grown-ups in Noisy Village have enough time to come and talk to him.

We told him precisely everything. He wanted to know a lot about the car, and Bosse could tell him every single thing about it. And I let Grandad hold my brooch in his hand. I told him it was full of small red jewels, and then Grandad said he could see it inside his head and that it was a beautiful brooch. Then I told him about the thing Monika's mum had said, that perhaps it was boring and humdrum in Noisy Village, and then Grandad said:

'Heh, heh, heh. Well, I never. To think folk can be so stupid!'

Grandad thinks exactly the same as me, that it's nothing but fun in Noisy Village.

I GET A LAMB

Spring is probably the best time of all. Anna and I always try to work out when it's most fun. Anna thinks it's most fun in the summer and I think it's most fun in the spring. And at Christmas too, of course. Anna thinks that as well.

Now I'm going to tell you about something that happened last spring. We've got masses of sheep here in Noisy Village and they have lambs every spring. Lambs are the sweetest things ever. They are sweeter than kittens and puppies and piglets. I almost think they are sweeter than Kerstin, but I daren't say that in case Olle hears.

When the sheep are lambing we usually run down to the sheep shed every morning to see how many lambs have arrived during the night. When you open the door of the sheep shed all the sheep bleat their heads off. The lambs sound so lovely and cute when they bleat, not croaky like the ewes and the rams. Almost every ewe has two lambs.

One Sunday morning when I went down to the sheep shed I caught sight of a lamb lying dead in the straw. I ran to Dad straight away and told him, and he went to find out why the lamb had died. It was because its mother didn't have any milk in her udder. That poor, poor lamb, he had died because he didn't get any food! I sat in the doorway of the sheep shed and cried. After a while Anna came and heard all about it, and she cried as well.

'I don't want lambs to die,' I said to Dad.

'No, no one wants that,' said Dad. 'But sadly enough here is another one that has to die.'

He showed me the tiny lamb that he was holding in his arms, and it looked so pitiful. It was the dead lamb's brother. Of course he couldn't get any milk from his mummy either, and milk is the only thing a new

10

born lamb can have. That's why Dad said we had to kill the dead lamb's brother so that he wouldn't have to starve to death. When we heard that, Anna and I cried even more. We cried an awful lot.

'I don't *want* lambs to die!' I howled, and threw myself on the floor.

Then Dad lifted me up and said:

'Don't cry, Lisa!' And then he said:

'I'll let you try feeding this lamb with a bottle, if you like. Just like a newborn baby.'

Oh, that made me so happy, happier than I think I have ever been before! I didn't know you could feed lambs like you do newborn babies. Dad said I shouldn't be too hopeful. He thought the lamb would probably die in any case, but we could always try.

Anna and I ran to Auntie Lisa, Olle's mum, and she let us borrow a bottle and a teat that Kerstin had drunk her milk from when she was really tiny. Then we ran back to Dad again.

'Dad, can't we give him some cream, the poor little thing?' I asked.

But Dad said that if I gave the lamb cream he would get ill. His tummy could only cope with milk that had been diluted with water. Dad helped me mix the milk and then we warmed the bottle in hot water. Then I pushed the teat into the lamb's mouth. And do you know what? He started sucking straight away. You could see he was hungry all right.

'So, now you are this lamb's foster mother,' Dad said. 'But he has to have food from the crack of dawn to late at night, so you mustn't get bored with doing it.'

Anna said that if I got bored with doing it I only had to tell her because she would love to feed the lamb for me. But I said:

'Ha! You needn't think anyone gets bored feeding lambs!'

I called the lamb Pontus, and Dad said it would be my very own lamb. It was lucky it was all decided before Lasse and Bosse woke up, otherwise there would have been a quarrel over Pontus, I'm sure of that.

'Honestly. You can't even have a lie-in without Lisa getting a lamb,' said Lasse, and he was a bit angry because it wasn't him who had been given Pontus.

At the beginning every single child here in Noisy

Village came to watch when I fed Pontus. But they soon got bored with it, every one of them.

It's really amazing how hungry lambs can be. They are hungry nearly all the time, it seems. Every morning before I went to school I ran down to the sheep shed and gave Pontus food. As soon as he saw me he came running up, wagging his short little stumpy tail and bleating so sweetly. He was white all over, but he had a small black patch on his nose so you could easily tell the difference between him and the other lambs. Agda gave him food once a day, when I was at school, but as soon as I came home I had to give him another meal. And late at night he had to have another one too. Once I tried getting Anna to go and feed Pontus for me, but she said:

'Tomorrow! I haven't got time today.'

But after all, I had promised Dad I wouldn't get bored with feeding Pontus and I didn't, either, because I loved him so very much. Most of all I loved him because he was so happy whenever he saw me. I expect Pontus thought I was his real mummy. But then Lasse said:

'Yes, I'm sure. You are so like a sheep.'

Then the day came when Dad told me I had to

13

try and teach Pontus to feed from a bowl, because he couldn't keep drinking from a teat until he was a grown ram, of course.

Poor Pontus, he had no idea why I came and put a bowl under his nose all of a sudden. He didn't know how he was supposed to drink. He nudged me with his nose to see where the teat was, and bleated so unhappily.

Bosse was with me, watching.

'Drink the milk, then,' he said to Pontus. 'Are you stupid? All you have to do is start drinking,' he said.

I got very angry with Bosse.

'Pontus isn't stupid at all,' I said. 'You don't know anything about lambs.'

As for Pontus, all he did was sniff the milk and bleat and be sad.

Anyhow, I understand lambs much better than Bosse because it was me who found the way to do it! I plunged my hand into the milk. And do you know what? Pontus started sucking my fingers. He sucked and sucked, and that way he slurped up all the milk. Well, a little got spilt, of course.

After that Pontus sucked my fingers for a time. But one morning he was really, really hungry and

couldn't wait for me to put my hand in the milk—
he started drinking anyway. And it worked out fine.
After that he never needed to suck my fingers. It
was a shame, actually, because he was such a darling
when he stood there sucking.

When it got warmer in the spring, the sheep were
let out to graze in our sheep meadow and the lambs
had to learn to eat grass. But they needed milk as
well, so I had to go to the sheep meadow every day
with my bowl of milk. When I got to the gate all
I had to do was stand there and shout 'Pontus!' as
loudly as I could. There would be a little bleat from
the farthest end of the meadow and Pontus would
come running up at top speed, his stubby little tail
wagging from side to side.

Now Pontus has grown so big that he doesn't get
milk any more. He eats grass and crunches leaves
and is so clever that I'm sure he will grow to be a big,
spectacular ram.

I might be given more lambs in my time, who
knows? Or perhaps dogs, or cats, or rabbits. But
none as sweet as Pontus. I will never, ever, *ever* like
anyone as much as I like Pontus.

PONTUS GOES TO SCHOOL

Lasse always teases me, and he used to say:

'It would be much better to have a dog than a lamb, anyway.'

Olle agreed with him of course, because Olle has got his own dog called Svipp.

'Oh yes, dogs are much better,' Olle said.

'And why is that, may I ask?' I said.

'Because you can take a dog with you everywhere,' Olle said. 'They follow you wherever you go.'

'Pontus just plods about over in the sheep meadow,' said Lasse.

'But a lamb is much sweeter,' said Anna, trying to help me.

'And what good is that?' said Lasse. 'When all he does is walk around in a sheep meadow.'

That was what we were talking about one day on our way home from school.

Next morning I went to the sheep meadow as usual and shouted for Pontus, and when he came running up all sweet and lovely, that's when I thought I wouldn't swap him for a thousand dogs. I thought of something else as well. I thought it was such a shame that all he did was walk around in the meadow where no one could see how sweet he was.

Sometimes Svipp runs after Olle all the way to school. I expect that was why Olle said that dogs follow you everywhere. Once our teacher let Svipp come into the classroom and lie down on the floor beside Olle's desk. Oh yes, Svipp was allowed! But poor Pontus, all he was allowed to do was wander around in the sheep meadow. He stood there, drinking milk out of his bowl, and I thought about how Lasse had sneered and how unfair it was that dogs could go everywhere but lambs couldn't. And by the time Pontus had finished his milk I had decided to let him come with me to school. That would shut Lasse up all right.

Our school is in Storby Village. It's quite a long way to go and we always walk together, all of us Noisy Village children. It was hard for me to be ready in time in the mornings when I had to go to the sheep meadow and feed Pontus first. On this particular morning, when I was going to bring Pontus to school with me, all the others were standing waiting for me outside Olle's gate.

'Hurry up, Lisa,' yelled Britta. 'Otherwise we'll be late!'

So I turned round to Pontus and yelled:

'Hurry up, Pontus, otherwise we'll be late!'

Never have I seen any children look as surprised as Lasse and Bosse and Olle and Britta and Anna did when they set eyes on Pontus.

'Where . . . where is he going?' Lasse asked.

'To school,' I said. 'So perhaps now you'll stop going on and on about how only dogs can go with you everywhere.'

They looked amazed, I can tell you.

'Lisa, are you quite sure you're feeling all right today?' asked Lasse.

'Do Mum and Dad know about this?' asked Bosse.

When Bosse asked if Mum and Dad knew about it, I got a bit worried. I hadn't thought about that. But Anna clapped her hands and laughed and said why shouldn't lambs be allowed to go to school the same as dogs. Yes, that was exactly what I was thinking! And all of a sudden Lasse began grinning sneakily, and he said:

'Let him come! Though our teacher will go doolally of course!'

So we trooped off down the hill. Pontus too. Sometimes he stopped for a moment, exactly as if he was wondering if this could be right. But all I had to do was call 'Pontus', and he would reply 'Ba-a-a' so cleverly, and trot to catch up with me.

It took a bit longer than usual to get to school, so we arrived late. The bell had already rung and the children had gone in. There aren't many of us children in Storby Village and Noisy Village so we all sit together in the same classroom and have the same teacher, even though we are in different classes.

Pontus stumbled as he went up the school steps, and I had to help him a little.

'Perhaps he's not ready for school yet,' Lasse said.

When Lasse started school a couple of years ago he couldn't sit still for a single minute. That's when our teacher said he wasn't ready for school yet. She sent him home and said he was to come back next year, because he had more playing to do. Lasse has never forgotten that, it seems. That's why he said what he did about Pontus.

Britta knocked on the door and we all stepped inside.

'Sorry we're late,' Britta said.

As soon as she said that, Olle started giggling. The rest of us were completely silent, but Olle went on giggling exactly as if someone was tickling him.

'Well, how very happy you sound today, Olle,' said our teacher.

Pontus was standing behind us, so no one could see him. But suddenly there was a sweet little 'Ba-a-a' and Pontus poked out his head. And all the children at their desks jumped. They really did. Our teacher too, of course.

'What on earth . . . ?' she said. 'You don't mean to tell me you have brought a lamb with you?'

'Lisa . . .' began Bosse, but then he stopped because I expect he thought our teacher would be cross with me. He wasn't the only one. I had started worrying about that too.

'Well, we are learning about domesticated animals at the moment,' I said, very quietly. 'So I thought . . .'

'What did you think?' asked our teacher.

'That it would be a good idea to see a real lamb, Miss,' I said. But I hadn't actually thought about it until that moment.

Our teacher laughed and laughed, and so did all the children. Especially Olle. The laughter really bubbled up out of him.

We led Pontus to the teacher's desk at the front and everyone was allowed to come and pat him. Then we talked about sheep in our lesson about the natural world, and I had to tell everyone how I had reared Pontus with a bottle. Everyone liked him very much, and we sang 'Baa Baa Black Sheep' to him. I think all the noise made Pontus tired and long to be back in the meadow, but he was good anyway, and stood very still beside my desk for the rest of the lesson. Except when he gave a little skip and a bleat. And each time he did that Olle started to laugh. He put his head down on the lid of his desk and just laughed and laughed, and that made everyone else laugh too.

When it's warm and sunny we always sit outside on the school steps to eat our sandwiches at break time. And that's what we did that day. As usual I had some milk in a bottle, and I gave it to Pontus. Our teacher let me borrow a bowl to pour it into. All the children thought it was fun to watch Pontus while he was drinking. Anna gave me half her milk so there was enough for me too.

Afterwards Pontus ran around the playground. He also decided he would like to nibble the carrot plants that had just started to grow in our teacher's vegetable garden. I shooed him away from there and told him he had to be patient and wait until he got home to the sheep meadow again.

When school was finished for the day and we were about to go home, Lasse said:

'Tomorrow we're going to learn about cattle. That'll be fun. I'll bring the bull with me.'

That made Olle laugh so much he got hiccups.

'Although of course it might be a bit squashed with him next to my desk,' Lasse said.

But our teacher said enough was enough and there would be no more live animals in school, even though it could be useful when we were studying the natural world. 'It can get a little complicated in the long run,' she said.

'Yes, because imagine what will happen when we start learning about crocodiles,' said Anna.

Then Olle burst out laughing and could just about manage to squeak:

'Then I'll bring in a crocodile!'

Pontus became very tired on the way home. We took it in turns to carry him up all the hills. Then we all took him to the sheep meadow together, and I have never seen a lamb scamper off and leap about like Pontus did when we let him into the sheep meadow. Honestly, he galloped off to the other sheep and bleated so much that you could hear it all over the meadow.

'It's very clear he isn't ready for school yet,' said Lasse.

ON OUR WAY HOME FROM SCHOOL

We always have such a lot of fun when we walk home from school, us Noisy Village children, because we talk about all sorts of things that have happened in school. And sometimes we tell each other stories or say what we're going to be when we grow up, and that sort of thing. Sometimes we sit by the roadside and have a little rest, and sometimes we climb trees or walk along the top of the fences instead of on the road, just so it doesn't get boring.

Mum says she can't understand why it takes us twice as long to come home from school as it does to get there. I don't understand it, either. It's odd, it really is. But it can't be helped. I don't think anything can be done about it.

One day last spring, when we arrived home particularly late, Mum said to me:

'Tell me exactly what you have been up to on your way home.'

And so I did. It was like this.

First we went to the shop in Storby Village and bought barley sugar for Grandad. Grandad likes barley sugar a lot, and we are only too happy to buy some for him because he keeps it in his corner cupboard and we're allowed to have some almost every time we go and see him. It was Britta who bought the barley sugar. It would have been very nice to taste some, but we knew we weren't allowed. Britta tucked it into her school bag and said:

'If six people taste the barley sugar then all that will be left for Grandad is the bag.'

'That won't do,' said Lasse. 'It's best we hurry home before there is an accident.'

We started walking homewards, but Bosse has such an awfully sweet tooth he said:

'If only I had one krona! Then I'd spend every bit of it on toffees.'

'Yes, but you haven't got one krona,' Anna said. 'It just so happens.'

'No, but what if we could find one?' Bosse said. 'If it just so happens.'

'And how would that work?' Britta asked. 'You always walk along staring right into thin air. You could at least look at the ground.'

So Bosse decided he would look at the ground. And he can't have gone more than fifty metres, I'm sure, before he found one krona! It was actually almost a miracle! Perhaps there are elves somewhere who hear what you wish for and go and spread one-krona coins along the road. This krona was lying exactly where the road turns off to Noisy Village.

At first Bosse only stood there staring at the coin, as if he thought it couldn't be true. But then he grabbed it and ran back to the shop and bought toffees, just like he had said. We waited by the roadside. And when he came back he offered toffees to all of us.

'To think finding money can be this easy,' Bosse said. 'We've missed out on loads of it!'

Oh, how we all stared at the ground after that! Lasse said:

'If only I had one krona!'

He thought perhaps an elf would give him one krona as well. But he didn't find a krona. Then he said.

'Think if I only had fifty öre!'

But he didn't find a fifty-öre piece. He didn't want to give up, so he said:

'Think if I had ten-öre!'

But he didn't even find that. Then he said irritably:

'I'll find a one-öre piece, you wait!'

But he didn't find one. Not Lasse, and not anyone else either. None of us has ever found as much as a single öre since that time Bosse found the one krona.

Bosse offered us toffees as we walked home. Then he came up with the idea that we should have a competition to see who could have a toffee in their mouth the longest before it dissolved. I expect he made that up so the toffees wouldn't be used up quite so fast. Anyway, we thought it was a good competition. We each put a toffee in our mouth and sucked as slowly as we could. And when a few minutes had passed we stood in a ring in the middle of the road and stuck out our tongues and compared, and there was almost nothing left of our toffees. We had come half way to Noisy Village by this time, and we were standing right outside Mr Gentle the shoemaker's cottage. The shoemaker stuck his head out of his kitchen window and said that if there was one of us with any sense left they could take Agda's newly-heeled shoes home to her. We quickly pulled in our tongues because no one was supposed to have been watching while we compared. Anyway, it was Britta who won the toffee-sucking competition. Lasse took charge of Agda's shoes and pushed them into his backpack.

Then Olle thought we should have a contest to see who could hold their breath the longest. So we did. But just to be on the safe side we waited until we had walked a little way past the shoemaker's house, because the shoemaker might have thought that was idiotic as well—standing in the middle of the road and holding our breath.

We held our breath for a really long time. I told Mum afterwards that of course that wasn't why we got home so late, but holding our breath for such a long time might have had *something* to do with it. Lasse insisted he had won, but then Olle said:

'Oh no you didn't. Bosse's face was much bluer than yours!'

Then Lasse said:

'What about seeing who can spit the furthest? But there's no point letting the girls have a go. They're useless at spitting.'

Britta and I got so angry. We can spit just as well as anyone else. Britta said that if we weren't allowed to take part in the spitting contest then the boys needn't bother coming to her birthday party the next day. Then we were allowed to join in. But of course Lasse won, though Anna definitely spat further than both Bosse and Olle.

The shoemaker owns a field that gets flooded every spring. When that happens it looks exactly like a small lake. There is a huge rock in the middle of the field. In the spring it sticks up out of the water just like an island. When we had walked as far as the shoemaker's field we stopped and had a rest for a while.

'I'd like to get out onto that rock,' said Lasse.

We all said that's what we wanted to do too. Lasse went and found a couple of fence posts which he put like a bridge over to the rock. And we crawled over one at a time, Lasse first. The weather was warm and sunny, and it was so lovely sitting there on the rock in the sunshine.

'If only we had something to eat,' said Anna.

But we didn't. The toffees had all gone. Then Lasse had a look inside his backpack. There were Agda's shoes and also a cheese sandwich which he hadn't managed to eat up at break time.

We pretended the rock was a ship that was drifting around in the ocean, and that we were sailors who were going to die of hunger any day if no one came to help us. Lasse divided the cheese sandwich into six equal pieces and gave them to us and said:

'Comrades, this is all that separates us from death. But be like your captain—be courageous!'

He was the captain, of course. Then he said the worst thing was that we had no water and so we would have to die of thirst as well. Then Bosse said:

'What are you talking about? The whole of the shoemaker's field is sloshing about with water!'

Then Lasse said Bosse was stupid. The water surrounding our vessel was salty and Lasse planned to shoot every single person who tried to drink it. Because if you drink salt water you go crazy, said Lasse.

Then he lay on the rock and pretended to be wailing with hunger and thirst, and Bosse said:

'Looks like he swallowed some salt water anyhow!'

Lasse knelt and clasped his hands together and shouted 'Help, help!' so that it echoed all around and felt really scary. And as he was shouting his loudest, who came running along but the shoemaker! He thought Lasse was really shouting for help and he was as angry as a raging bull.

'If you got yourselves out there then you can get yourselves back,' he said. 'Blessed kids.'

But he waded out into the water anyway and lifted us down from the rock one by one and threw us back onto dry land again. It's true he was wearing wellington boots, and it's also true that he told us off non-stop, but it was kind of him to save us all the same. Although quite unnecessary. But we didn't dare say that, of course.

We hurried away from there. He shouted after us that he was so tired of Noisy Village kids, he was more tired of us than anything else, and next time we should leave his fence posts alone.

After we had been walking for a while I happened to look at Lasse's backpack, and then I said:

'Agda's shoes! What did you do with those?'

Lasse looked horrified. He said the shoes were still on the rock, of course. He had put them there while he looked for the cheese sandwich. We turned around, all of us, because we thought it would be a shame for Lasse to have to go back on his own.

Yes, there were the shoes all right, still on the rock, wrapped in newspaper. But the shoemaker had taken away the fence posts. Since it was so warm and sunny Lasse thought we should all take off our shoes and socks and wade out to the rock. So we did. It wasn't that cold in the water at all. We pretended the rock was a wreck that had run aground, and that we were pirates who had to climb aboard to rescue precious treasure—Agda's shoes, that was. But we pretended the wreck was full of other pirates who were guarding the treasure, and we ran around in the water and shot at the other pirates. Lasse gave the commands and we climbed up onto the wreck with our knives between our teeth—well, they were sticks really, but we pretended they were knives. And at last we were all up on the rock and Lasse swung Agda's shoes above his head and shouted:

'The plunder is ours! Death to each and every one who approaches us now!'

Then the shoemaker appeared. It was none other than him walking towards us. Poor thing, I felt really sorry for him when he caught sight of us, because now he realized that he had saved us for no reason. He gawped and said nothing, and his mouth hung open for ages. And we sat in absolute silence on the rock. But eventually the shoemaker came to life.

'Clear off!' he roared. 'Clear off, before I do something I'll regret!'

And we hopped down from the rock and splashed ashore and picked up our shoes and socks and ran away from there as fast as we could. The shoemaker shouted after us that it was very strange there was nowhere in Noisy Village where we could go and make a noise.

We went home. We didn't stop any more. Well, apart from looking at a bird's nest in a tree that Bosse knew about, that is. We climbed up one at a time and looked at it. There were four small, light blue eggs in it. Bosse had eggs like that in his collection. But Bosse is very careful about birds and birds' nests. And we looked ever so carefully. It didn't take such a long time.

But when I told Mum all about it, she said:

'Now I'm beginning to understand why it's impossible for you to get home from school before five o'clock every day.'

Lasse went to Agda and said that she would have her newly-heeled shoes tomorrow. He had them in a very safe place, he said. She didn't have to worry at all that they might disappear overnight because they were on a shipwreck and being guarded by pirates. And by a very angry shoemaker.

OLLE HAS A LOOSE TOOTH

One day our teacher said to Olle:

'Why are you sitting there with your fingers in your mouth, Olle?'

Olle looked very embarrassed. He said:

'I've got a loose tooth.'

'Pull it out when you get home, then,' said our teacher. 'At the moment we are doing arithmetic. Tomorrow we'll all be able to see the gap where the tooth was.'

Then Olle looked ever so frightened, because he

thinks it's nasty pulling teeth out, however loose they are. I think so, too.

'Oh, pulling out a little milk tooth like *that* isn't going to hurt,' Dad says.

It might be true that it doesn't actually hurt that much, but it's horrible at any rate. We usually get 10 öre for every one of our teeth Dad pulls out. He only pulls out the loose ones, I mean, but that's bad enough. Seems to me there's always a loose tooth. Bosse isn't scared at all of having a tooth pulled out. So he shouldn't really get 10 öre, if you ask me. All he does is tie a piece of extra strong thread around his tooth, tug it sharply and pop, out it comes. But Dad gives Bosse 10 öre anyway, because he is so brave.

But Olle, poor thing, he gets even more scared than I do when he has to have a tooth out. We all had a feel of his wobbly tooth as we walked home from school. And it was really wobbly.

'I can whip that out easy as anything,' Bosse said.

'You're not whipping out anything round here,' Olle replied. He walked with his head down all the way home and didn't say much.

'Oh, you mustn't be upset about a loose tooth.

That's nothing,' I said, because it's only horrible when you've got a loose tooth yourself.

'I know what we'll do,' Lasse said. 'You tie some thread around it when we get home and then we'll tie the other end to the fence, and then I'll heat up an iron bar until it's red hot and then I'll wave it about under your nose. You'll get so scared you'll jump backwards and the tooth will fly out.'

'You and your stupid iron bar,' said Olle angrily. He didn't think it was a good idea at all. But anyway he did tie some extra strong thread around his tooth when we got home, so that he could pull on it occasionally and make the tooth even looser. He simply *had* to try and get it out somehow, because our teacher wanted to see the gap the next day. That's what she had said. And I think that was what troubled Olle most of all—his tooth had to be out by the following day. Otherwise our teacher would know that he was afraid of having a tooth pulled out, and Olle didn't want her to know that.

Anna tried to comfort him. She said:

'Oh well, she might have forgotten about your tooth by tomorrow.'

But Anna knew as well as Olle that our teacher almost never forgets anything. People with a good memory can be trouble, Lasse says.

We played rounders down by the road, like we usually do on spring evenings, and all the time there was a long black thread hanging out of Olle's mouth. It looked so funny when he was running. From time to time he must have forgotten about the tooth and the thread and how worried he was because he laughed and talked as usual. But then all of a sudden he would look miserable and strange, and pull anxiously on the thread and sigh.

'It's seven o'clock now and you still haven't pulled out that tooth,' Lasse said at last. 'Don't you think we should try that iron bar after all?'

Bosse asked to look at the tooth again, and then he said:

'Are you barmy? It's only hanging on by a pathetic little shred of skin! Pull it out, why don't you!'

Olle shuddered when he heard that, because it's just that last little shred of skin that is so difficult.

When we got tired of playing rounders we went

up to see Grandad. We told him that Olle had a loose tooth.

'He's got to pull it out this evening,' Lasse said. 'Because our teacher wants to see the gap tomorrow.'

'Heh, heh, heh,' said Grandad. 'Heh, heh, heh, that's teeth for you! When I was a lad . . .'

'Yes, Grandad, tell us about when you were a lad,' Anna said, and climbed up onto his knee.

And so Grandad told us that when he was a child he had terrible toothache for a whole month, and in the end he was forced to go to the blacksmith to have the tooth pulled out. There was no dentist where they lived in those days. The blacksmith took a big pair of pliars and pulled out Grandad's tooth, and it hurt so dreadfully. But when Grandad got home he still had terrible toothache, because the blacksmith had pulled out the wrong tooth. Grandad had toothache for another whole month and he didn't dare go back to the blacksmith because it hurts so badly to have large back teeth pulled out with a normal pair of pliars. But in the end he had such horrible toothache that he *had* to go back. And this time the blacksmith pulled out the right tooth.

But he had to bend his elbow and practically hang from his pliers, Grandad said, because the tooth sat so firmly and had such big roots.

'Poor Grandad,' said Olle. But I think he thought his own tooth was just as awful to get out, even though it had no roots at all.

'To think, Grandad, that you have been a little child and scared of having teeth pulled out,' said Anna.

'Heh, heh, heh, that was long ago,' Grandad said. 'Now I only have three teeth left and them'll drop out on their own any day.'

'So now you don't have to be afraid any more,' Anna said, happily.

'No, no, my dear, now I don't have to be afraid any more,' Grandad said.

Then he went over to the corner cupboard and took out barley sugar for us. He gave us each a clump and said:

'Don't eat barley sugar! It'll give you toothache! Heh, heh, heh!'

Then we said goodnight to Grandad and went away.

'So what about your tooth, then?' Lasse asked Olle. 'Is it going to sit there until you are as old as Grandad?'

Olle got angry, and I'm not surprised.

'Is it bothering you?' he said. 'It's my tooth, you know!'

'Yes, but when are you going to pull it out?' asked Britta.

Olle played with the thread and said:

'Tomorrow. First thing. Maybe.'

Then he ran off home, poor thing. Lasse said:

'It's a shame about Olle. I know what I'm going to do. When Olle has gone to sleep I'll climb into his room and pull his tooth out.'

'No—o—o!' we said. 'You can't do that.'

'Oh, yes I can,' Lasse replied. 'Dentist Lars Eriksson—teeth extracted with general anaesthetic,' he said, strutting about. Lars is Lasse's real name.

Then we said we wanted to go with him and watch. So we all ran up to Lasse and Bosse's room and sat and waited.

All three houses in Noisy Village are built very close together. There are only a couple of metres between South Farmhouse where Olle lives and Middle Farmhouse where we live. A linden tree grows right in the middle between them and Lasse and Bosse and Olle always climb through the tree when they want to visit each other. Olle's room is precisely opposite Lasse and Bosse's room, where we were sitting waiting.

We heard Olle doing something in his room. Finally Lasse shouted:

'Are you still up, Olle?'

'Well, you're still up,' Olle shouted back.

'No, Bosse and I are lying down,' shouted Lasse. And we giggled quietly because although they really were lying down, it was on the floor of course, and they were still dressed.

'Aren't you sleepy, Olle?' shouted Bosse after a while.

'Yes, but you're shouting so much I can't sleep,' answered Olle.

So he must have gone to bed after all, we hoped.

'Turn your light out, Olle,' shouted Lasse.

'Turn your own light out, why don't you?' Olle shouted back. So Lasse did.

We sat there in the darkness and waited. After a little while Olle switched off the light in his room.

'Please let him fall asleep soon, otherwise *I* will,' said Anna, yawning.

Just then we heard rustling outside in the linden tree. It was Olle coming over. Britta and Anna and I darted into the wardrobe. Lasse and Bosse threw themselves into their beds and pulled the covers right up to the chin.

'Know what, Bosse,' said Olle, as he stuck in his head. 'I might not be well tomorrow and won't be able to go to school. In that case you don't have to wait for me.'

'Not well? Why would you be not well?' asked Lasse. 'If only you went to bed on time every night you'd be as fit as a fiddle.'

'I've got a tummy ache,' said Olle, and climbed back to his own room.

I'm positive he only had a tummy ache because he was so nervous about his tooth.

We waited a long, long time and in the end we were so tired we could hardly keep our eyes open.

'He must have fallen asleep by now,' Lasse said finally.

So he climbed out into the linden tree.

'Are you awake Olle?' he said, as softly as he could.

'No, I'm asleep now,' said Olle.

So we had to sit and wait a bit longer. But finally Lasse said he thought he would go over and see if Olle had fallen asleep, because if he hadn't then he really *was* ill, and Lasse would go and get the doctor for him. So then we all climbed through the linden tree as silently as we possibly could. Lasse had his torch with him. He shone it on Olle's bed, and there lay Olle with the thread hanging out of his mouth. Oh, I got so scared! I felt exactly how nasty it was to have a tooth pulled out. Think if it hurt so much that Olle started screaming! And what would he say when he saw all of us standing there?

Lasse took a firm grip on the thread and said:

'One two three,
On the fourth slap your knee,
On the fifth tap your nose,
On the sixth bang it goes!'

And just as he said 'sixth' he tugged—and there was the tooth, dangling from the thread. And Olle hadn't even woken up. He only mumbled in his sleep and said:

'I've got such a tummy ache.'

Bosse tried to wake him up but he couldn't. Then Lasse said that was a good thing, because then Olle would think a ghost had been there and pulled out the tooth for him. Lasse tied the thread from the ceiling light and the tooth dangled there. It would be the first thing Olle saw when he woke up in the morning. Imagine how happy he was going to be!

Olle most definitely did not have a tummy ache the next day. He stood outside his gate, waiting for us as usual. And he was laughing so much you could see a big gap in his top gum.

'Was it you Lasse, who did it?' he asked Lasse.

And then we told him that we had been in his room, all of us. Olle laughed even more when he heard what he had said in his sleep. He was so happy that he jumped about and kicked every stone lying in the road. Then he said:

'Actually, it's not that difficult, having a tooth pulled out.'

'No, not when you have an anaesthetic,' said Lasse.

And we decided that we would all pull each other's teeth out at night—well, the wobbly ones, that is.

When we arrived at school Olle went straight to our teacher, opened his mouth gaping wide and said: 'Look, Miss, I've pulled my tooth out.'

'You mean I have, more like,' muttered Lasse from his desk. But our teacher didn't hear that.

Even Anna and I don't really know what we're doing

Anna and I have a special place behind the outhouse where the first blue wood anemones grow, and we have another place where other spring flowers grow. And all the woods and meadows in Noisy Village are simply covered with white wood anemones. We pick the wood anemones and the other spring flowers, and if you hold the bunches under your nose then you know it's spring, even with your eyes closed.

Anna and I have got another spring place as well. It's in a deep ditch. We've got two wooden boxes that we sit on. The water rushes all around us but we don't get wet, at least not much. All around the ditch the hawthorn bushes grow all close together, so where we sit it's exactly like a green room of leaves. We sit there in the ditch quite often. When the hawthorn is in bloom and the sun shines and the water rushes around us, then it's such a good spring place, I think. But Britta doesn't understand that. One day last spring while we were sitting there, Anna and me, Britta came and stuck her nose through the bushes. She caught sight of us down in the ditch and then she said:

'What are you doing?'

Anna and I looked at each other and thought.

'We don't really know ourselves what we're doing,' I said.

Because we didn't. Then Britta went off, saying that if you didn't know yourself what you were doing then it couldn't be worth doing, and you might as well be doing something else. But Anna and I stayed there, even though we didn't know what we were doing.

Golden saxifrage flowers grow in that ditch, and all of a sudden I said to Anna that I was Princess

Golden Saxifrage. And then Anna said that she was Princess Cowslip.

'Welcome to my green palace,' I said.

'And welcome to *my* green palace,' said Anna.

Then we almost fell out for a little while over whose green palace it actually was. But then we came up with the idea that Princess Saxifrage and Princess Cowslip were twins and each had their own part of the palace.

'O, my green palace,

O my rushing river,' said Anna, in that pretend voice she puts on when only she and I play together.

And I also said:

'O, my green palace,

O, my rushing river.'

I picked sprigs of hawthorn and put them in my hair. And Anna did the same.

'O, my white, white flowers,' I said, and I thought Anna would probably say the same. But she didn't.

'O, my white, white . . . rabbits,' she said.

'What do you mean, rabbits?' I asked.

'My enchanted rabbits,' Anna said. She said she had a golden rabbit hutch with two small enchanted rabbits in her palace.

'Ha, ha, *you* haven't,' she said.

But at that moment I saw a little frog sitting on the edge of the ditch, and I said:

'O, my enchanted little frog!'

And I caught the frog quickly because every single person knows that frogs are mostly princes under a spell. In fairy tales, I mean. Anna knew that too, and she became so envious of me because of my frog.

'Oh, can I hold him for a little while?' she asked.

'Hold your white rabbits, why don't you?' I answered.

But Anna begged and pleaded to hold my frog for a while, and so I let her.

'Think if it really is a prince under a magic spell,' said Anna.

'That hawthorn has gone to your head,' I said.

But then I started thinking. Perhaps the scent of the hawthorn flowers was so strong in the sunshine that it had gone to my head as well, because all of a sudden I thought, *who knows*, it could be an enchanted prince. In those days, when princes were turned into frogs, I expect there were also *ordinary* frogs that weren't princes at all. Then it could easily happen that an enchanted prince was forgotten because people thought it was just an ordinary frog. And if no princess had bothered to give him a kiss, then he would have to stay a frog for all eternity, even after the fairy tale came to an end. Poor thing. And here he was sitting in a ditch in Noisy Village, left behind. I asked Anna if she thought that too, and she did.

'Well, then' I said. 'There's only one thing to do. We must kiss him, to break the spell.'

'Ugh,' said Anna.

But I said that if princesses in olden times had been as silly and pathetic as she was then we would to this day have ditches full of enchanted princes.

'Yes, but we're not real princesses, are we?' Anna insisted.

'We've got to try, at least,' I said. 'If we do it together it might work.'

'You start, Princess Golden Saxifrage,' said Anna, and handed me the enchanted prince. I held him in my hand and looked at him, and when I thought about having to kiss him my stomach turned over. But it couldn't be helped.

Then I thought of something.

'Know what, Anna,' I said. 'If this really is a prince under a spell, remember that the frog was mine.'

'What do you mean by that?' asked Anna.

'You know, if he's going to have the princess and half the kingdom.'

But that made Anna angry.

'If I help out and kiss him, then he's just as much mine as yours,' she said. 'Let him make up his own mind!'

And so we decided that the prince would be allowed to choose for himself whether he wanted Princess Golden Saxifrage or Princess Cowslip. Then I said:

'One two three,
On the fourth slap your knee,
On the fifth tap your nose,
On the sixth bang it goes!'
And I shut my eyes and kissed the frog.

'He's probably under a very strong spell,' Anna said, when no prince appeared. 'I really don't think there's any point in me kissing him.'

'Oh no you don't,' I said. 'Here you are, Princess Cowslip.'

So then she took the frog and kissed him very, very quickly. But she was in such a hurry that she managed to drop the frog in the ditch and it hopped away as fast as it possibly could.

'You ninny,' I said. 'There goes our enchanted prince.'

'You know what?' Anna said. 'I think you need to be a real princess to make it work with those ugly things.'

Then we heard a loud burst of laughter from behind the bushes. And there stood Britta and Lasse and Bosse and Olle. They had seen and heard everything.

'Look, here are the girls who don't even know what they're doing,' said Britta.

And Lasse rolled his eyes and said:

'O, my green palace,

O my rushing river,

O, my white, white flowers!'

'O, my white, white rabbits,' said Bosse.

'And then the frog had half the kingdom and half the princess,' said Olle, doubling over with laughter.

Then Anna picked up an empty can that we had

in the ditch, filled it with water and hurled it straight at Olle.

'Are you mad!' shouted Olle. 'What *are* you doing?'

'I'm so angry I don't know what I'm doing,' said Anna.

And I cupped my hands in the ditch and threw the water right into Lasse's ear.

'No, Anna and I don't really know what we're doing,' I said.

THE WISE MEN'S CASKET

That tooth—the one Lasse pulled out of Olle's mouth—might as well have been a nugget of gold the way Olle looked after it. He kept it in a matchbox in his pocket and he took it out from time to time to look at it.

A couple of days later Bosse had a loose tooth. It wouldn't have been any trouble at all for him to pull it out by himself like he usually did, but now Bosse had got it into his head that he also wanted his teeth pulled out while he was asleep. That's why he tied a piece of extra strong thread around his tooth in the evening, before he got into bed, and tied the thread to the door handle. And when Agda came upstairs the following morning to wake the boys up, she pulled open the door and the tooth flew out and Agda didn't need to try and wake Bosse up.

'It's absolutely incredible how much fun you can have with teeth,' said Bosse, as we were going to school that day. He had also put his tooth in a matchbox, and Olle and Bosse walked along comparing teeth. It irritated Lasse that he didn't have a pulled-out tooth. But he said:

'I wonder where I put my molar that was taken out when the dentist came to Storby Village last year.'

That evening he searched through his drawer really thoroughly and found many fine things he thought were lost forever. In a cigar box lay some horse chestnuts and several empty rifle cartridges and a broken whistle and five broken tin soldiers and a broken propelling pencil and a broken watch and a broken torch and also his own molar. That was broken too. That was why he had to have it taken out. Lasse looked at all his broken things and said he was going to mend them when he had the time. Well, not the tooth, of course. He put that in a matchbox. And all evening Lasse and Bosse and Olle went around rattling their matchboxes and showing off, and they didn't want to play rounders, not even once. Britta and Anna and I played hopscotch and ignored them.

'I'm so tired of teeth I'll spit my own out soon,' said Britta.

Just then the boys turned up. They had been in Bosse and Lasse's room for a long time, and they were looking very sly.

'Don't tell the girls, whatever you do,' said Lasse.

'Not likely. That would be just perfect if we told *them*, I don't think,' said Bosse.

'Out of the question,' said Olle.

We were so curious we could have burst, Britta, Anna and me. But we knew what was going on so we said nothing.

'It's your turn now, Anna,' I said.

And we played hopscotch for all we were worth and pretended we weren't curious.

Lasse and Bosse and Olle sat at the side of the road and watched.

'You did hide it, didn't you?' Bosse said to Lasse.

'Rest assured,' said Lasse. 'The Wise Men's Casket has to be hidden in a safe place.'

'Yes, because otherwise the girls could get hold of it,' said Olle. 'And that would be a disaster.'

Lasse pulled a face, as if he couldn't think of a worse disaster.

'Don't say such terrible things, Olle,' he said. 'If the girls were to get hold of it . . . oh dear, oh dear!'

'It's your turn now, Lisa,' said Britta.

We played hopscotch and pretended we hadn't heard a word about the Wise Men's Casket.

Then the boys left. All three walked in single file along the road, and Anna pointed at them and whispered:

'There go the three wise men, hee hee!'

And we laughed as hard as we could. Lasse turned round and said:

'It's good you're keeping cheerful, even though there are one or two things you haven't got a clue about, you poor things.'

That's when we decided we would look for the Wise Men's Casket. Of course, we knew it was one of the boys' usual stupid inventions, but even so we did want to know what the Wise Men's Casket was.

The boys had gone off to the paddock to ride Svea, our black mare, so we headed off to Lasse and Bosse's room. And searched. Oh, how we searched. But it isn't easy to find the Wise Men's Casket when you don't even know what it looks like. We looked in the chest of drawers and under the beds and on the shelves in the wardrobe and everywhere in the attic. But no Wise Men's Casket did we see.

As we were in the middle of our search we heard the door of the attic stairs open and the boys come clattering up. Oh, how we had to rush! There are masses of clothes hanging in the attic and we tucked ourselves behind them and stood very, very quietly.

'Let's get it out and have another look,' said Bosse.

'First we'll find out where the girls are,' Lasse said. 'Perhaps they're in Lisa's room playing silly games with their dolls.'

'No, because then you'd hear them jabbering, wouldn't you?' said Olle. 'They're down at North Farmhouse, I bet. Get out the casket!'

We stood there, not daring to move. I was so afraid I would need to sneeze or that I would start laughing. It looked like Lasse was going to bump straight into me, and I thought oh no, I'm going to die! But he stopped in time and bent down, and lifted out something I couldn't see. Anna nudged me and I nudged her back.

'Wise men, swear that you will never reveal the hiding place,' said Lasse.

'Yes, but what do we say?' asked Bosse.

He doesn't find it as easy as Lasse and me to make things up. But Olle said:

'We swear never to reveal the hiding place.'

'Swear never to let the Wise Men's Casket fall into the hands of the heathen,' said Lasse.

It was Britta and Anna and me who were the heathen, of course, and I nudged Anna again.

Bosse and Olle swore never to let the Wise Men's Casket get into the hands of the heathen.

'Because you see, if the heathen get their hands on it, it will lose its secret power,' said Lasse.

Oh, I so wanted to see that wonderful casket, but the boys were standing in the way. Eventually Lasse put it back under the loose floorboard and then they thundered down the stairs again.

Oh, didn't we move! As soon as the attic door slammed shut we rushed over and lifted up the floorboard. And there was the Wise Men's Casket. But wait till I tell you! It was nothing but Lasse's old cigar box. WISE MEN'S CASKET it said in capital letters on the lid, and underneath was a drawing of a skull.

'Hurry up and open it, Britta, so we can see what the special thing is inside,'

So Britta did. Anna and I stretched our necks as far as we could to be able to see. And what we saw were only three little white teeth. Two tiny ones and one a bit bigger. That was all there was inside the Wise Men's Casket.

'Sometimes I wonder if boys are all right in the head,' said Britta.

Agda, who helps Mum, keeps all her things in an old chest of drawers up in the attic. Mum has said that on no account are we to touch Agda's chest of drawers. But Agda is so kind. She always shows me lots of lovely things she keeps in her chest of drawers.

She has a little pink pin cushion with lace round the edges and lots of beautiful postcards with flowers on and a bottle of perfume that smells gorgeous and a bracelet which is practically gold and . . . well, there is so much I can't list it all.

When the dentist was in Storby Village last year he made a new set of false teeth for Agda because he said he had never seen such ugly false teeth as her old ones, and it was a pity to have such teeth when otherwise you looked so nice, he said. But Agda didn't throw away that old set of false teeth. She told me she might wear them on weekdays sometimes, at least when the weather was bad, and save the new ones for Sundays.

'Those old teeth will do well enough to go and feed the pigs and milk the cows,' she said.

But she soon grew tired of the old false teeth because the new ones looked much more beautiful. Agda likes Oskar, our farmhand, so I expect she wants to look nice on weekdays too.

The old set of false teeth lay in Agda's top drawer, I knew that. And now I had such a brilliant idea.

'Do you know what we can do?' I said to Britta

and Anna. 'We can put Agda's old false teeth in the Wise Men's Casket. If the boys' three useless little teeth can magic up secret power, what wouldn't you get with a full set?'

Britta and Anna were very happy with my suggestion. It was much better than stealing the Wise Men's Casket, said Britta. Because when boys think up such stupid ideas, you have to show that you're not taking them seriously, she said. Womenfolk really cannot take part in any kind of foolishness, she said.

So we put Agda's teeth in the cigar box and put the box back in its place. Then we went out to look for the boys. They were down on the road, playing marbles. We sat on the roadside and watched.

'Ah, I see the wise men are playing a game of marbles late in the day,' said Britta.

They didn't answer. Lasse had his hands full of marbles, and I said:

'The Wise Men's Casket would be a good place to keep marbles, I would have thought.'

They still didn't answer. But Lasse sighed deeply. You could tell he thought the heathens were being more stupid than normal.

'Oh go on, you can tell us about the Wise Men's Casket,' said Anna, giving Lasse a shove.

But then Lasse said it was nothing you could tell girls. The Wise Men's Casket was full of secret power. You could work miracles with it. The Casket was in a secret place, he said, and we would never, ever, *ever* know where. Only the secret brotherhood that was responsible for the casket could know where it was. Otherwise it would lose its power, said Lasse.

'The secret brotherhood, is that you and Bosse and Olle?' asked Britta.

Then Lasse kept quiet and looked mysterious. But Britta and Anna and I started laughing as hard as we could.

'I think they're annoyed because they don't know where we keep the cigar b—I mean, the Wise Men's Casket,' said Bosse.

'You're keeping it in your wardrobe, of course,' said Britta, very cunningly.

'Yes, well, for your information we're not,' said Bosse.

'Oh no? Well, in that case, you've got it under a loose floorboard in the attic,' said Anna.

'Oh no we haven't!' said Lasse and Bosse and Olle all together. But oh, how worried they looked! They forgot where they were in their game of marbles.

'Shall we go and look at your birds' eggs, Bosse?' said Lasse.

Look at Bosse's birds' eggs—and he thought we would fall for that! We understood well enough that they were going to go and rescue the Wise Men's Casket.

'My birds' eggs? Oh, you've seen them so many times,' said Bosse, who can be a bit slow occasionally. But then Lasse glared at him angrily and finally Bosse understood.

'Oh, of course you can come and look at my birds' eggs,' he said, looking very crafty.

So the boys walked away—slowly, so that we wouldn't suspect anything. But then we had to hurry. We ran to Olle's mum and told her we were only going to fetch something from Olle's room, and then we raced up the stairs and climbed through the linden tree over to Lasse and Bosse's room and out into the attic, and hid ourselves behind the clothes.

And no sooner had we got there than the boys came clumping up the stairs.

'What do you think Anna meant about the attic floor?' said Bosse.

'Huh,' said Lasse. 'That was just something she thought up. But it's probably best we move the Wise Men's Casket to another place, to be on the safe side.'

So Lasse removed the floorboard, but we couldn't see anything because the boys were blocking our view.

'Open it, so I can have a look at my tooth,' said Olle.

'And I want to see mine,' said Bosse.

'Wise men,' said Lasse. 'That which lies hidden in this casket may never be seen by the heathen. Only by us.'

Then it went quiet, and we realized that Lasse had lifted the lid. And they must have seen Agda's teeth because all we heard was a yell. And we leapt out from behind the clothes and laughed. And I said:

'Now you've seen enough secret power to last for a whole year.'

Then Lasse threw Agda's teeth across the attic floor and said girls shouldn't exist because they only destroy everything.

Anna said:

'Go on, Lasse, do some miracles with the cigar box!'

'Are you asking for a thump?' said Lasse.

But then Lasse and Bosse and Olle threw their teeth away and we all went outside and played rounders.

LASSE CATCHES PREHISTORIC OXEN

There are two things that make me envious of Anna and Britta. The first is Grandad. Grandad says that seeing as there are so few children here in Noisy Village, he might just as well be Grandad to all of us. But then Anna says:

'Maybe so, but really, really, *really* you are my Grandad. And Britta's too, of course.'

When we are up at Grandad's, reading the newspaper to him, then it's always Anna who sits on his lap, and he calls her sweetheart all the time.

I can't understand for the life of me how he can tell the difference between Anna and the rest of us, when he is almost blind. But he can. And Anna isn't even hairy like that Esau in the Bible story. It was as easy as anything for Esau's dad to tell the difference between his children, when one of them was hairy and the other wasn't. But Grandad is really clever, I think, seeing as Anna isn't a bit hairy.

Anyway, Grandad is kind to all of us, so actually it doesn't matter so much that he calls Anna sweetheart.

But Britta and Anna have got their own lake too. That's the second thing I'm envious about. You only have to run across their cow meadow and you get to North Farm Lake. That's where we go swimming in the summer. It's got such a lovely beach. Once, when we had a quarrel, Anna said I wasn't allowed to swim in their lake. But then Anna's mum said I could swim there as much as I wanted. Because that was the law, she said. So Anna can't forbid me from swimming in North Farm Lake, however much we have quarrelled. Most of the time we are friends, by the way.

On the other side of the lake there isn't a beach.

There are high cliffs there. At least, *I* think they are high, but then Lasse says I should see the Rockies. We usually pretend they *are* the Rockies, those cliffs on the other side of the lake. We row over there sometimes in North Farm's rowing boat.

Lasse says it must have been a giant who hurled all those large blocks of stone and boulders about in the Rockies. Long, long ago, when there were no people. And no Noisy Village. I'm glad I wasn't alive then, when there was no Noisy Village. It certainly was lucky that someone decided to build Noisy Village. Lasse says that in those days we would have had to live in the cave in the Rockies. There is a really brilliant cave there, under a couple of huge, huge blocks of stone.

There's a pine tree where we usually tie up the boat when we go over to the other side of the lake. Then we climb straight up the rocks. But not just any old how. We have special places we know we can grab hold of. And we need them, I can tell you, with something as difficult as rock climbing. We've got a crevice we call the Nose Grazer. That's because it's so narrow you almost always graze your nose when you

70

climb through it. You *have* to climb through there because it's the only way. Then there's a rock that juts out, and you have to step onto a narrow little ledge to get past. We call that rock the Arm Breaker. That's because Lasse says that once Bosse fell down from there and practically broke his arm off. Bosse says he didn't do that at all—well, yes, he did fall down, but he only *grazed* his arm, and Lasse deserved a bashing for saying that he almost broke it. But the rock is called the Arm Breaker anyway. The most dangerous place of all is called Dead Man's Hand. If you fall down there you'll have to be carried home in a wheelbarrow, Lasse says. But once you have managed to get past all those difficult places then you are nearly up on the highest rock. And then if you walk a little way into the forest you come to our cave. We call that cave Massive Cavern.

One Sunday last spring, just before school broke up for the holidays, we went on an outing to the Rockies. We had a packed lunch with us and told everyone at home that we would probably be gone all day.

Lasse tied the rowing boat to the usual pine tree,

and then we started climbing. We talked about what was most fun—climbing rocks or climbing trees. And we thought, all of us, that it was probably a tiny, tiny bit more fun climbing rocks. We made up a new place and called it Tummy Squidge, because you have to squidge in your tummy to get past there. Well, the place wasn't new, of course. We had climbed past Tummy Squidge many times before. But then we didn't know it was called Tummy Squidge.

When we had to climb over Dead Man's Hand I shivered, because it was so exciting. Mum could never have seen Dead Man's hand because otherwise she wouldn't have let us play in the Rockies. Lasse looked down into the depths and said:

'Anyone planning to fall down there raise a hand or a foot!'

We certainly couldn't raise any hands or feet because we needed those to cling on with. But no one fell down and soon we were at Massive Cavern.

There is a beautiful glade in the forest right next to Massive Cavern, and there we spread out our packed lunch. You always get hungry immediately when you're on an outing. And we thought, all of us, that it was just as well to eat straight away. We had small pancakes and jam with us, and milk and juice and sandwiches and biscuits. Olle had brought dumplings, six of them. The idea was to have one each, but we couldn't eat cold dumplings when we had such a load of pancakes. Anna and Britta had brought kringles, little cakes that their mum makes and are ever so nice. We all had a taste of those. Finally there was only one kringle left, and Bosse really, really wanted to have it, because he loves cakes.

Olle was a bit angry because no one wanted to eat his dumplings. And I suppose Britta must have felt sorry for him, for she said:

'You can have the kringle, Bosse, if you eat up Olle's dumplings.'

Bosse was quite full up already, but he tucked in anyway because he did so want to have the kringle. He swallowed the first dumpling in one bite. And the second one disappeared pretty quickly too, although a little slower. He sighed as he started on the third one, but Britta held the kringle in front of his nose and he managed to stuff that one down as well. Then he began on the fourth one. He took a bite and said:

'The frorth is on its way down!'

'You dope,' said Lasse. 'It's not called the frorth, it's called the fourth.'

'I'm so full up I don't even know what *I'm* called,' said Bosse.

Anna hopped about on one leg, shouting:

'One two three,
On the fourth slap your knee,
On the fifth tap your nose
On the sixth bang it goes!'

'I think I'm going to go off bang any minute,' said Bosse, and he didn't want to eat any more dumplings.

'You get the kringle anyway,' said Britta.

But Bosse said he was never going to eat a kringle again in his life, and never, ever, *ever* any dumplings.

Then we went into the cave. Lasse said that people might have lived inside it in the Stone Age. Ugh, how cold it must have been for the poor things in the winter! There were great big cracks between the rocks where the snow could blow in.

Britta thought we should pretend to be those Stone

Age people, and Lasse thought that was such a good idea. He said that he and Bosse and Olle would go out and hunt down prehistoric oxen and tame them. Britta and Anna and I were to sit at home in the cave and keep the food warm. Well, isn't that strange! Whatever we play, the boys always do the fun things, but all we get to do is keep the food warm and things like that. But Britta said we could take some twigs and sweep the cave and wedge a few pretty branches of birch leaves in the cracks to make it homely.

Lasse said: 'Do what you like, even if it's silly! Come on lads, let's go and catch a prehistoric ox!'

But Bosse was so full of dumplings that he couldn't do a thing, and he said he didn't have the energy to hunt any prehistoric oxen.

'Well then, you might as well stay at home in the cave and shout at the women and children,' said Lasse. 'The main thing is that you've got something to do.'

'I'd like to see him try,' said Britta.

But as for Bosse, he was so full up that he lay down on the grass outside the cave and that is where he stayed the whole time, while Lasse and Olle were out hunting prehistoric oxen and we were sweeping the cave. Then Lasse and Olle came back and let out the most terrifying howl, just so we could hear how well the hunting had gone, Lasse said. I've heard Lasse make a lot of noise in my time, but nothing like that sound. Lasse said it was a prehistoric howl and that it was the sound people made when they hunted prehistoric oxen in the Stone Age. He showed off enormously about how dangerous it was, hunting prehistoric oxen, and said he had caught masses. But we didn't see any.

Then it started to rain and we sat inside the cave and had such a nice time. The sky had turned very dark and we thought that was the end of the good weather for the day. But all of a sudden the sun came out from behind a cloud. That's when we saw how lovely the island looked in the middle of North Farm Lake. The sun was shining on the flat rocks where we sometimes swim. And Lasse said:

'What about rowing over there to go swimming!'

It can't have been more than two days since we asked Mum if we could start swimming soon, but Mum had said:

'No, it's too early. You'll still have to wait a while!'

'Now we *have* waited a while,' said Lasse.

And so we rowed over to the island. We took off our clothes by the flat rocks and had a competition to see who would be the first into the water. It was Bosse. It seemed the dumplings had gone down a little bit.

It was so terribly cold in the water that we were soon out again. And the first thing we saw when we got out was North Farm's angry ram. He stood there with his big curly horns, looking very threatening. North Farm's ram can't be in a field with the other sheep because he leaps over all the paddock fences and gores everyone he sees. Every spring he is usually put out on the island all on his own. It's a horrible job trying to get him there. Uncle Erik and Dad and Uncle Nils all help to tie his feet with rope, and then they lay him down in North Farm's rowing boat, and Uncle Erik rows him over to the island and sets him free there. But we were so startled when we came up out of the water and saw the ram standing on the beach, glaring at us, because we had forgotten he was there. The ram's name was Ulrik.

'Oh my goodness gracious!' screamed Anna. 'To think I forgot about Ulrik!'

I'm sure Ulrik thinks it's really infuriating being

tied up like that, and being put in a boat while his wives and all their little lambs are watching. Perhaps that's why he is so angry. And then of course it's very boring walking about on the island all alone.

Now it seemed he was more angry than usual. He lowered his head and set off towards us, butting his head in all directions. Olle was butted and that made him fall over, but he got up on his feet fast and ran for his life. We all did. Bosse and Anna and Britta climbed up on a high rock, Olle and I climbed into a tree, and Lasse hid behind a bush.

I shouted at Lasse:

'You're so clever at catching oxen! Here's one for you—well, almost. Let's see how you catch him.'

And Britta and Anna shouted:

'Yes, here comes the prehistoric ox, Lasse. Catch him now!'

But Lasse didn't dare answer, standing there behind the bush, just in case Ulrik heard he was there.

Ulrik was angry because he couldn't get at us with his horns. He stood under the tree where Olle and I were sitting and butted the trunk so much that smoke came off the bark. And when that didn't help he went over to the rocks where Bosse and Britta and Anna had climbed up. He stood underneath and stared at them as hard as he could.

'You can stare,' said Britta.

Eventually we began to wonder how we were going to get away. Ulrik didn't look as if he was getting tired of watching us.

'If only I had a dumpling,' said Bosse.

We had hidden the left-over dumplings back at Massive Cavern and we'd forgotten to bring them with us. And now, when Bosse started talking about dumplings, we all realized how hungry we were.

'Have you fallen asleep behind that bush?' Olle shouted to Lasse.

Then Lasse stuck out his head and looked around. He tried to creep towards the rocks where Bosse and Anna and Britta were sitting. But he should never have done that. Ulrik caught sight of him and gave a jump of delight. He set off towards Lasse. Lasse ran and we screamed. It looked so awful, Lasse tearing around the juniper bushes with Ulrik hot on his heels.

'Run, Lasse, run!' shouted Anna.

'That's exactly what I *am* doing,' Lasse shouted back.

Ulrik knocked Lasse over once and we screamed so much it sounded like the prehistoric howl. It seemed the howl scared Ulrik a bit. Lasse got up and ran on. Ulrik set off after him and we screamed even more. But it didn't help.

There is an old hay barn on the island. The roof is broken and it isn't used any more. The door stood wide open and Lasse ran inside. Ulrik followed. Then I started crying and I said:

'Oh, now Ulrik will gore Lasse to death inside the barn.'

But suddenly we saw Lasse come climbing up through the broken roof. Then he hopped down onto the ground and ran and shut the door with Ulrik inside, and said:

'The prehistoric ox has been trapped.'

At last we dared to get down, and then we all climbed up and looked at Ulrik through the broken roof. Bosse spat at Ulrik and said:

'Shame on you, you ugly old ram!'

And I said:

'I hope Pontus never turns into an angry old ram like you!'

Then it was time to go home. Lasse told us all to get into the rowing boat. As for him, he was going to open the door for Ulrik and then race to throw himself into the boat before Ulrik understood what was going on. Because even though Ulrik was a stupid angry ram, he couldn't be left shut in the barn to starve to death, Lasse said.

We did as Lasse told us. We always do.

As we rowed away from the island Ulrik stood on the beach looking as if he thought it was very sad that we were leaving.

'Let me know if you want any more prehistoric oxen captured,' said Lasse, and he was so smug.

But we didn't want any more prehistoric oxen captured that day. We were so tired and hungry that all we wanted to do was get home.

'I'll ask Mum if she's got any dumplings,' said Bosse.

WHEN IT'S MIDSUMMER IN NOISY VILLAGE

Perhaps Anna is right after all, and we do have most fun in the summer. Except I like going to school, and when our teacher says goodbye to us on the last day of the summer term it almost makes me cry, because I know I can't see her for such a long time. But I soon forget that because it really is lovely having summer holidays.

On the first evening of our summer holidays we usually go down to North Farm Lake to fish. There is almost nothing that feels as summery as fishing. We have made a fishing rod each. It's only a long hazel branch, but we've got real fishing line and floats and sinkers and hooks that we bought in the shop in Storby Village.

Lasse calls the evening we finish school the Great Fishing Evening. There is a heap of rocks just the right size where we usually sit and fish. It's called Perch Mountain. It's called that simply because you never catch any perch there, says Anna. The only things you do get are mosquito bites, she says. But Bosse caught a big perch last time we there, anyhow, and Britta got two small roach.

Anna and I sat on our kitchen doorstep afterwards and counted mosquito bites. I had fourteen on my right leg and five on my left. Anna had nine on each leg.

'You could almost use it as an arithmetic question,' said Anna. 'We'll have to write it down on a piece of paper for our teacher. "If Lisa has fourteen mosquito bites on one leg and five on the other, and Anna has nine on each leg, who has got the most bites and how many are there all together?" '

But then we remembered it was the summer

holidays, and how silly it was to spend time doing sums. So we just scratched our mosquito bites and had a lovely time right up until we had to go to bed. Oh, how lovely the summer holidays are!

And now I'm going to tell you what we did when it was midsummer. We always had a midsummer maypole at South Farmhouse. Everyone in the whole of Noisy Village helped to make it. First we rode on our hay wagon a long, long way into the forest and picked birch branches to decorate the maypole. Dad drove. Even Kerstin was allowed to come along. It made her very happy and she laughed. Olle gave her a little branch of leaves to hold and she sat and waved it about. And Olle sung that old song for her:

> 'Kerstin had a gilded coach
> And in it she would ride
> A gilded whip was in her hand
> To greet the folk on each side.'

Actually, we all sang. Agda also came with us to cut branches, and she sang:

'Now it's summer
And the sun is shining
Now there are flowers and leaves

But then Lasse sang like this:
Now it's summer
And the sun is shining
Now there's cow poo in the field.'

Well, he was right, I suppose. About the cow poo
in the field. But you don't necessarily have to make
up a song about it.

When we got back from the forest, Agda and
Britta and Anna and me went and cut masses of lilac
that grows behind our wood shed. Then we took it to
South Farm meadow. And there Oskar and Kalle had
already made the maypole. Kalle is the farmhand at
North Farm. We decorated the maypole with birch
leaves and tied two large wreaths of lilac to it. And
then we raised the maypole and danced round it.
Uncle Erik, Anna's dad, can play the accordion so
well. He played lots of funny tunes that we danced to,
all of us. All except Grandad and Kerstin. Grandad

sat on a chair and listened. At first Kerstin sat on his lap, but then she wouldn't stop pulling his beard so her dad came and lifted her up onto his shoulders. That meant Kerstin could join in the dance as well. But poor Grandad couldn't dance, of course. But I don't think that made him sad. All he said was:

'Heh, heh, heh, it were a while since I did any dancing round a maypole!'

Then we all sat down in the grass to drink the coffee that Mum and Auntie Greta and Auntie Lisa had made. We had buns and biscuits too. Grandad drank three cups of coffee. He *loves* his coffee.

'Can't do without my drop of coffee, that I can't,' says Grandad.

I don't like coffee at all, but when it's midsummer and you drink it on the green grass, then it tastes so much better than usual.

There was a bird singing and singing in the forest while we drank our coffee. Bosse said it was a blackbird. I like blackbirds.

We played games too. Last Couple Out, and all sorts. It's such fun when the mums and dads join in the games. Well, it wouldn't be quite so much fun if you had to play with them every day, I mean. But when it's midsummer I think they can join in. Svipp raced around and he thought it was fun as well.

We were allowed to stay up as late as we liked that evening. Agda said if you climbed over nine paddock fences before you went to bed, and picked nine kinds of flowers and put them under your pillow, then you would have a dream that night about the man you were going to marry.

Britta and Anna and I thought it would be fun to climb over nine fences, even though we had already decided who we were going to marry. I'm going to marry Olle, and Britta and Anna are going to marry Lasse and Bosse.

'So you're going to climb over nine fences?' said Lasse to Britta. 'Well, go ahead. And dream about someone else, if you don't mind. Not that I believe in superstition, but it *might* help.'

'We can always hope so,' said Bosse.

'Yes, we can *really* hope so,' said Olle.

You see, the boys are so stupid that they don't want to marry us.

Agda says you have to be absolutely quiet when

you climb over the fences. You're not allowed to laugh or keep talking all the time.

'If you're not allowed to talk all the time,' said Lasse, 'then you might as well go to bed now, Lisa.'

'Why?' I asked.

'Well, it's impossible to climb over nine fences in two minutes. And you've never been quiet for longer than that. Apart from when you had mumps, that is.'

We paid no attention to the boys and set off to do our climbing.

We started with the paddock fence at South Farm and came out in the woods behind it. Oh, how strange it is in the woods when it's dark. Well, it wasn't completely dark, but nearly. And it was so silent because the birds had stopped twittering, and there was a lovely smell of trees and flowers. We each picked a flower when we had climbed over the first fence.

There is one thing I don't understand. Why is it that you feel you are bursting with laughter precisely when you know you mustn't laugh? As soon as we had climbed over the first fence, it started. And

Lasse and Bosse and Olle came climbing after us, to tease us and trick us into laughing.

'Don't step in the cowpats,' Bosse said to Anna.

'There aren't any cow . . . ' said Anna, but then she remembered that she was not supposed to talk. Then we started giggling, Britta and Anna and me. And the boys laughed.

'You mustn't giggle like that,' said Lasse. 'You're not allowed to laugh, remember.'

Then we giggled even more. And the boys ran around us all the time, pulling our hair and pinching our arms just to make us laugh. And we couldn't tell them off, of course, because we weren't supposed to say anything.

'Ubblybubblypoo,' said Lasse.

That wasn't the tiniest bit funny, actually, but oh how we laughed at it, Britta and Anna and me. I stuffed my handkerchief into my mouth, but that didn't help because the laughter came squeaking out anyway. But by the time we had climbed over the ninth fence we stopped laughing and only felt angry with the boys for spoiling everything for us.

But I put my nine flowers under my pillow anyway.

There was a buttercup and a harebell and a daisy and meadow saxifrage and clover and a wild rose and three other flowers. I don't know their names. But I didn't dream of anything at all that night. I'm sure that's because those stupid boys had tricked us into laughing.

But I expect I'll marry Olle in any case!

THE CHERRY COMPANY

We've got so many cherry trees here in Noisy Village, in our garden and Anna and Britta's garden. There aren't any in Olle's garden, at least not with nice cherries growing on them. But instead the South Farmhouse family have one tree that has delicious pears and two that have lovely little yellow plums on. Outside Grandad's window is the biggest cherry tree in the whole world, I think. That tree is called Grandad's cherry tree. The branches hang almost all the way down to the ground and every year it is full of huge cherries. Grandad says we can eat as many cherries as we want. But we mustn't pick the cherries from the lowest branches because those are for Kerstin, Grandad says. He wants Kerstin to be able to go and pick them herself. And she can do that too, even though she is so little. But Olle has to keep an eye on her or she'll eat the stones as well. We do what Grandad tells us. We don't take any of the cherries from Kerstin's branches. After all, it's so easy for us to climb up into the tree and eat them there. There are so many good branches and places where you can sit and eat. You can stuff yourself full of cherries for precisely as long as you like—or at least until you have a tummy ache. We get a bit of a tummy ache every year when it's cherry time. But then we don't get tummy ache again until the plums are ripe.

Lasse and Bosse and I each have a cherry tree which is our very own. My cherry tree isn't very big but it has such scrummy small black cherries. This year it was unbelievable how many cherries there were. And it was the same with Lasse and Bosse's trees too.

You can dry cherries and keep them for the winter. Mum always does that. She spreads them on drying trays and puts them in the oven when it's hardly hot at all. Then the cherries go dry and crinkly and you can keep them as long as you like, and make fruit soup in the winter.

When we had so many cherries on our trees it was impossible for us to eat them all up, even though Britta and Anna and Olle helped. Lasse thought he would dry some cherries one day and he filled a whole tray and put it in the oven. Then he went swimming and forgot all about them. The next time he looked at his cherries all he saw was a few blackened and sad little crumbs on the tray.

'That's no way to treat cherries,' said Lasse.

Then one evening we sat with Grandad, reading the paper to him, and in the paper it said that in Stockholm cherries cost two kronor a litre. It made Lasse incredibly annoyed that his cherry tree wasn't in Stockholm.

'If it was then I'd stand on a street corner and sell cherries and be as rich as the king,' he said.

We tried to work out how much money we would have if our cherry trees were in Stockholm. It came to such an awful lot that Lasse almost turned white at the thought of it.

'If I had North Farm Lake in the Sahara then I could sell lake water for two kronor a litre too,' said Britta, because she thought Lasse was stupid.

But I think Lasse lay awake at night thinking about how you could get two kronor for a litre of cherries in Stockholm, because the next day he said he was planning to open a cherry shop down by the main road that runs behind Storby Village. Lots of cars drive past on that road.

'And who knows, some of those crazy Stockholm people might come along,' said Lasse.

Bosse and I said we wanted to sell our cherries too. We set up a business that we called The Cherry Company. Britta and Anna and Olle were allowed to be a part of it too, even though they didn't have any cherry trees of their own. But they helped us pick our cherries.

We got up at five one morning and started picking, and by the time it was almost eight we had all the cherries in three big baskets. Then we ate plenty of porridge, to last us a long time. After that we set off down the hill to Storby Village. When we got there we went to Uncle Emil in the shop and bought a load of brown paper bags with the money we had borrowed from Bosse's piggy bank.

'What are you up to now?' asked Uncle Emil.

'We're going to sell cherries,' said Lasse.

We had left the baskets on the steps outside. Olle was guarding them.

'Mm, cherries. Lovely,' said Uncle Emil. 'May I buy some, perhaps?'

Well, that was lucky! Lasse went out and fetched one of the baskets, and Uncle Emil picked up a one-litre measuring can. He measured out two litres for himself and gave us two kronor for it. He said that was the price of cherries in this area, and it's lucky we found that out, of course. Bosse was given back the money we had borrowed from his piggy bank, and we still had money left. Uncle Emil gave us sweets, and when Olle saw that through the glass in the door he came rushing in as if his pants were on fire. But after he had been given his sweets he rushed out again just as fast.

We thanked Uncle Emil very much and left. When we got outside we saw that Olle was picking up some cherries that had fallen out onto the grass.

'What are you *doing*?' shouted Lasse angrily.

'I'm . . . I'm only sorting through your cherries,' said Olle, and he sounded very frightened.

But it was scarcely more than one or two he had spilled, so it didn't matter.

The main road isn't far from Storby Village at all. In the autumn and winter you don't see an awful lot of cars there. Only lorries, really. But in the summer lots and lots of cars come along this road, because people want to see how beautiful it is here.

'That's if they can see anything at all, the way they drive,' said Lasse, as the first car whizzed past.

We had made a big sign which said DRIVE-BY CHERRIES, and we held it up as soon as a car came along. But the cars only drove straight past. Lasse said the people in the cars probably thought our sign said DRIVE CHEERFULLY, or something like, which is why they speeded up so suddenly. As for Bosse, he loved watching the cars drive by so fast. He almost forgot about the cherries. His eyes were big and round in his face, and he stared and stared as they drove past. He knew the make of every car. He sat down by the roadside and pretended he was driving a car and he made the noise of an engine. Suddenly he said there must be something wrong with the engine because it didn't sound the way it should.

'No, that's because it doesn't sound a bit like an engine. It only sounds like Bosse,' said Britta.

Lasse was cross because the cars wouldn't stop, and he said:

'Right, I'll show them!'

When the next car came along he jumped out into the middle of the road and held up the sign, and he only leaped out of the way at the very last second. The car stopped with a terrible squeal and a man jumped out and took hold of Lasse's arm and said he deserved a good thrashing.

'Don't ever do that again,' he said.

Lasse promised not to. And guess what, the man bought a litre of cherries from us, and then he went on his way.

There was so much dust flying about on that road. We had covered the cherries over with paper, and that was probably very sensible of us. But we couldn't cover ourselves, and when the cars drove past they left a thick cloud of dust behind them, and all the dust fell on us. It wasn't very nice, and I said:

'Ugh, this dust is so horrible!'

Then Lasse asked me why I had said that.

'Why don't you say: "Ugh, the sun is shining!" or "Ugh, the birds are twittering!"' Lasse wondered. Who had decided that you had to like it when the sun shone but not when there were clouds of dust? So then we made up our minds that we would like the dust. And when the next car sped past and all the dust blew over us so we could hardly see each other, Lasse said:

'Oh, how beautiful the clouds of dust are today!'

And Britta said:

'Yes, this is such a very dusty road—how nice it is!'

And Bosse said:

'If only we could have more clouds of dust.'

Well, he certainly didn't have long to wait. A huge lorry came driving by and there was more dust thrown up by that lorry than I ever thought possible. I think it must have been like one of those pillars of cloud the children of Israel had in the desert. Anna was standing right in the middle of the very worst of the dust and she stretched out her arms and said:

'What wonderful, wonderful dust!'

But then she had to cough and couldn't say anything else. When the dust had settled we looked at each other and we were grey, all of us, big as we were. Britta blew her nose and then she showed us her handkerchief and it was completely black where she had blown it. And so we all blew our noses and we had black snot, every one of us. Bosse didn't have a handkerchief with him, so he blew his nose in Bosse's. But Britta said it wasn't so easy to see if Olle had black snot because his handkerchief was black from the beginning, she said.

'Oh, get lost,' said Bosse.

Even though there was so much lovely dust we thought it was sad anyway that none of the cars wanted to stop. But eventually Lasse realized that we had been standing on a very silly part of the road, right in the middle of a straight stretch where the cars were travelling very fast. We ought to move to a bend in the road instead, he said. So we did. We stood a little further along, where there were two tight bends in the road, one right after the other. We came up with the idea of standing in a row alongside the road, holding hands and swinging our arms up and down whenever a car came along.

'That'll do the trick,' said Lasse.

And it did. Almost every car stopped. The first one had a dad and a mum and four children in it, and all the children shrieked for cherries. Their dad bought three litres of cherries, and their mum said:

'Oh, this is such good luck! We are so hungry and thirsty!'

It was my small black cherries they bought. The dad told me they would be travelling far, far away overseas. Well, how very strange that was! To think my cherries would travel all the way abroad while I stayed here at home in Noisy Village. When I told the others, Lasse said:

'Huh, don't you know those children will have eaten up all the cherries long before they leave the country?'

But I said my cherries were going abroad anyway, even if it was inside the tummies of those children.

Oh, we sold so many cherries! One man bought a whole basketful. That was the basket with Bosse's cherries. The man said his wife was going to make cherry cordial, because he was very keen on cherry cordial.

'Strange, isn't it?' said Bosse afterwards, just to tease me. 'To think my cherries are going to be cherry cordial, but I'm not going to be cherry cordial myself!'

Eventually we had sold every single cherry. And there was thirty kronor in the cigar box we had brought with us to keep the money in. It was the Wise Men's Casket that had finally come in really useful. Thirty kronor! That was an absolutely humungous amount of money! We shared it out so we had five kronor each, because even if Britta and Anna and Olle hadn't contributed any cherries of their own, they had helped to pick them and sell them, at least.

'And now you haven't got any cherries of your own left, you can eat as much as you like from our garden,' said Britta.

'You can have plums from me as soon as they're ripe,' said Olle, when he was given his five kronor.

So it was shared out fairly and no one can say any different.

On the way home we went into the bakery in Storby Village and each bought a cake and some lemonade. We could afford to do that. The rest of the money we would save. There was green marzipan on my cake and it tasted scrummy.

When we got home and Mum caught sight of Lasse and Bosse and me she clapped her hands together and said a dirtier cherry company she had never seen. She wanted us to go to the outhouse and wash ourselves, but just then Anna came along, yelling:

'What luck! The sauna is hot!'

The North Farm family have a Finnish sauna down by the lake. We took clean clothes and hurtled like lightning through the meadow.

In the sauna we washed off all that lovely dust. We held out our bowls of water and compared whose water was dirtiest. But you couldn't see any difference.

Then we sat in the sauna and had a good sweat. And while we did that we talked about how we might have a plum company as well, soon.

It is very hot in the sauna and finally we were so hot we thought we would explode, so we raced out into the lake to cool off. Oh, how good that was! We splashed each other and swam and dived. And when we came out there was none of that lovely dust left, not even in our hair. We blew our noses in the water, too, to get rid of all the black snot.

It was such beautiful weather. We sat by the side of the lake and sunbathed. And Lasse said:

'Ugh, the sun is shining so much!'

And then Olle laughed and said:

'Ugh, the birds are singing so much!'

ANNA AND I WANT TO BE NURSERY NURSES
—PERHAPS

One day the vicar in Storby Village was having a big birthday party and everyone in Noisy Village was invited. Well, not the children, of course. But Mum and Dad, Uncle Erik and Auntie Greta, and Uncle Nils and Auntie Lisa were invited. And Grandad as well. Auntie Lisa was sad because she thought she wouldn't be able to go because of Kerstin. Someone had to look after Kerstin, you see. But then Anna and I said we could look after her. We were going to be nursery nurses anyhow, when we grew up, so it was just as well we started practising as soon as possible.

'But is it really necessary for you to practise on my little sister?' asked Olle.

I expect he wanted to look after Kerstin himself, but he had to milk the South Farm cows and feed the pigs and chickens while his mum and dad were at the party. Britta probably also wanted to help look after Kerstin, but she had an awful cold and was in bed and could hardly speak.

Auntie Lisa was so happy when she heard that we wanted to look after Kerstin for her. And Anna and I were even happier. I pinched Anna's arm and said:

'Isn't it going to be fun?'

And Anna pinched me back and said:

'If only they would go soon so we can get started.'

But it always takes such a very long time before people leave for a party. Not Grandad, though. He was ready at six o'clock in the morning, even though they weren't going to set off until ten. He was wearing his smart black clothes and his best shirt. As soon as Uncle Erik had hitched the horses Grandad went out and sat in North Farm's cart and waited, before Auntie Greta had even started putting on her party frock.

'Grandad, don't you think it will be fun going to a party?' asked Anna.

Grandad said he did. But I think he felt it was going to be more trouble than fun, because all of a sudden he sighed and said:

'Heh, heh, heh. I don't know, all this going out to parties!'

Then Uncle Erik said it was five years since Grandad went to a party, so he wasn't the one to complain about parties.

Auntie Lisa was giving us instructions right up to the very last minute, and then Dad and Uncle Nils and Uncle Erik clicked the horses and off they all went.

Auntie Lisa said we had to let Kerstin be out of doors as much as possible because then she behaved better. That's what Auntie Lisa said. But at twelve o'clock she had to have her food, which was all ready to heat up. And then we had to put her down for a nap for a couple of hours.

'Oh, this is going to be such fun!' said Anna.

'Yes,' I said. 'And I'm definitely going to be a nursery nurse when I grow up, that's one thing I know for sure.'

'Me too,' said Anna. 'It's not a bit hard looking after children. You only have to remember to talk to them nice and gently. That makes them obedient. That's what it said in the newspaper the other day.'

'Yes, well of course you have to talk nice and gently,' I said.

'Oh, believe you me, there are people who scream at their children,' said Anna. 'But those children end up as complete tearaways and never obey at all! It said so in the paper, so there!'

'Who would want to scream at a little darling like this?' I said, tickling the sole of Kerstin's foot.

Kerstin was sitting on a blanket in the grass, looking happy. She is very sweet, is Kerstin. She has such a round little forehead and her eyes are so blue. In her mouth she has four teeth at the top and four at the bottom, and when she laughs they look just like grains of rice. She can't speak yet. The only thing she can say is 'Lo, lo,' which is her way of saying hello, hello, and she says it almost all the time. She might mean different things each time, you never know.

Kerstin has a wooden cart that she's usually pulled around in.

'What about taking her for a little ride in the cart?' suggested Anna.

And so we did.

'Come along, little Kerstin,' said Anna, and she put her in the cart. 'Come along, let's go for a ride.'

She spoke so nice and gently, just the way you should talk to little children.

'There you are, little Kerstin. It's nice sitting there, isn't it?' she said.

But Kerstin didn't think so. She wanted to stand up straight in the cart and jump up and down and say 'Lo, lo'. But we didn't dare pull her along like that.

'I think we're going to have to tie her down,' I said. So we found a thick piece of string and did just that. But when Kerstin couldn't jump up and down and say 'Lo, lo' she started yelling her head off so that it could be heard for miles around. Olle came rushing down from the barn, saying:

'What are you doing? Are you hurting her?'

'Of course we're not hurting her, you dope,' I said. 'And we are talking to her nice and gently, if you must know!'

'Well carry on doing that,' said Olle. 'And let her do what she wants, then she won't cry.'

Yes, Olle knows best how his sister should be looked after, so we let Kerstin stand up straight in the cart and say 'Lo, lo' as much as she wanted. I pulled the cart and Anna ran beside it and caught Kerstin every time she fell out. And that's how we did it. But then we came to a deep ditch and when Kerstin saw it she climbed out of the cart.

'Let's see what she wants to do,' said Anna.

And we saw all right! There is something very strange about little children. You think they can't run fast on their small legs, but that's wrong. If necessary a little child can run faster than a rabbit. At least, Kerstin can. She said 'Lo, lo,' and shot right down into the ditch before we had time to blink. Then she tripped and landed on her head in the water. Now, Olle had said she was allowed to do exactly as she wanted, and perhaps she wanted to lie in the ditch, but we thought it was probably best to pull her out anyway.

She was wet all over and screamed and glared so angrily at us, exactly as if it was our fault she had fallen in. But we talked to her nice and gently and sat her in the cart and pulled it back home to put dry clothes on her. She howled the whole time. Olle was so angry when he saw what Kerstin looked like.

'What are you actually doing?' he shouted. 'Have you tried to drown her?'

Then Anna said he should speak nice and gently to us, because we are children too. Though quite big ones, of course.

Kerstin toddled up to Olle and wrapped her arms around his legs and screamed and wanted to be comforted, so Anna and I felt exactly as if we *had* tried to drown her.

Olle helped us find clean clothes for Kerstin, but after that he had to go down to the barn again.

'Sit her on the potty seeing as she's got her clothes off,' he said before he went. I wonder if he has ever tried to sit Kerstin down himself. In which case it would have been fun to see how he went about it. Anna and I used all our strength to push Kerstin down on the potty, but it was useless. All she did was make herself as stiff as a stick and shout to high heaven, and not sit down.

'Stupid kid,' I started to say, but then I remembered that wasn't the way you should speak to little children.

Because Kerstin didn't want to sit on her potty there was nothing for it but to put the dry clothes on her anyway. I held her arms while Anna tried to dress her. Kerstin screamed the whole time and was as slippery as an eel and threw herself from side to side, and it took us half an hour to get her ready. Afterwards we each sat down on a chair, completely exhausted. But Kerstin stopped screaming and said 'Lo, lo' and crawled under the kitchen table and made a little lake there. Then she stood up and dragged the table cloth down, so that two coffee cups crashed to the floor and broke.

'Horrible child,' said Anna, as nice and gently as she could. She wiped the floor under the table and picked up the pieces of broken china, and I took off Kerstin's wet knickers. While I was looking for another pair Kerstin decided to scamper off. She was through the door and half way to the barn before we caught hold of her. Then Olle stuck his head out of the barn doorway.

'Are you mad?' he shouted. 'Are you letting Kerstin go out with no knickers on?'

'No, that's not what we're doing,' said Anna. 'She hasn't actually asked us, if you want to know!'

We dragged Kerstin indoors and put dry knickers on her, but she wriggled this way and that, and shouted the whole time.

'*Now . . . will . . . you . . . please . . . behave . . . and . . . stand . . . still,*' said Anna. She said it *more or less* nice and gently, but not really.

Kerstin was wearing her best dress, because Olle hadn't been able to find another one. It was so pretty. It was white with small neat tucks and gathers.

'You must be careful with that dress,' I told Kerstin, although of course she doesn't understand yet what you say to her. You can certainly tell that. I mean, that she doesn't understand what you say.

'Lo, lo,' she said, and ran straight into the fireplace and got a big patch of black soot right in the middle of her dress. We brushed it off as best we could, but it didn't go all that well. Kerstin laughed very happily while we were brushing her. She must have thought we were playing with her.

'It's twelve o'clock,' said Anna suddenly. 'Time for Kerstin to have her food.'

We hurried to heat up the spinach that was in a saucepan on the stove. Then I sat Kerstin on my lap and Anna fed her. She ate very well and opened her mouth beautifully, and Anna said:

'She's a very good little kid really.'

Then Kerstin said 'Lo, lo,' and hit the spoon, and all the spinach flew in my eyes.

Anna laughed until she nearly dropped the dish.

That made me start to get angry with her. Kerstin laughed too, but I don't expect she knew what Anna was laughing at. I'm sure Kerstin thinks it's completely natural for people to have spinach in their eyes.

All of a sudden she didn't want to eat any more. She clamped her lips shut and kept shoving the spoon away so that more than half the spinach fell onto her dress. We gave her fruit soup to drink from a cup, and half of the fruit soup landed on her dress as well. So then the dress wasn't white any longer, but green and red instead, and only a little bit white in certain places where she hadn't managed to spill spinach or fruit soup.

'If there's one thing I'm very pleased about,' said Anna. 'It's that this kid is going to have her afternoon nap now.'

'Yes, I'm very pleased about that too,' I said.

So we struggled to get Kerstin's clothes off again and put on her sleepsuit, and by the time we had done that we were completely worn out.

'If anyone needs an afternoon nap, it's us,' I said to Anna.

We put Kerstin in her cot in the little room beside the kitchen and went out and shut the door. And that's when Kerstin began to scream her head off. We tried to pretend we didn't hear her, but she screamed louder and louder and in the end Anna stuck her head round the door and said:

'Shut up, you horrid kid!'

Obviously you have to talk nice and gently to little children, but sometimes it doesn't sort of work. Although what it said in the newspaper was probably right, about children turning into tearaways if you shout at them. Kerstin, at least. She just screamed and screamed, worse than before. So then we both went in to see her, and instantly she became happy and stood up in her cot and jumped up and down and said 'Lo, lo.' She carried on like that the whole time we were in there with her. She stuck her little hand out between the bars of her cot and patted me and rested her cheek against mine.

'She's a sweetheart, really,' I said.

Then Kerstin bit my cheek, and I had a mark there for two days afterwards.

We laid her down in her cot again and tried to tuck the blanket around her. She kicked it off again immediately. After she had kicked it off ten times we stopped bothering about it. All we said was: 'Sleep tight, little Kerstin,' and we went out and shut the door. And hey presto, she started screaming to high heaven again.

'No, that's enough now,' said Anna. 'Let her scream!'

And we sat at the kitchen table and tried to chat. But it didn't work, because Kerstin screamed louder and louder and louder. It almost made you start sweating when you heard it. Sometimes it went silent for a couple of seconds, but that was only when she was building up for the next howl.

'Perhaps she's got a pain somewhere,' I said at last.

'Oh yes, what if she's got a tummy ache,' said Anna. 'It could be her appendix or something.'

And so we *ran* into Kerstin's room. She stood up in her cot and her eyes were full of tears, but as soon as she saw us she said: 'Lo, lo,' and began jumping up and down and laughing.

'That child hasn't got a pain in her tummy or anywhere else either,' said Anna. 'Come on, let's go.'

So we shut the door on Kerstin and threw ourselves down at the kitchen table again and sat there sweating and listening to Kerstin's screams getting worse and worse. But finally it did go silent anyhow.

'Oh, how lovely,' I said. 'Now she's fallen asleep at last.'

And Anna and I took out Olle's game of Ludo and sat there and played Ludo and had a really nice time.

'Little kids should be in their beds all the time, then at least you know what they're up to,' said Anna.

At that very moment we heard a strange sound coming from the room. It sounded like a contented little murmur, the kind small children make when they are doing something that's fun.

'No, this is going too far!' I said. 'Surely the child can't *still* be awake!'

We crept up and peered carefully through the

116

keyhole. We saw Kerstin's cot. But no Kerstin. The cot was empty. Then we rushed into the little room beside the kitchen, which was newly white-washed and lovely for the summer. It *had* been lovely, I mean. Before Kerstin got to it. Now it was not quite so lovely because Kerstin was sitting in the middle of the fireplace holding a tin of shoe polish. She was black with polish all the way from the top to the bottom with only small patches of whitewash in between. She had shoe polish in her hair and shoe polish all over her face and shoe polish on her hands and on her sleepsuit, and the entire stove was decorated with shoe polish. Probably Uncle Nils had been standing by the fireplace polishing his shoes before he set off for the party, and not put the lid on afterwards.

'Lo, lo,' said Kerstin, when she saw us.

'Did it say in the newspaper whether you were allowed to slap little children or not?' I asked.

'I don't remember,' said Anna. 'My head is absolutely spinning.'

Then Kerstin stood up in the fireplace and came towards us and wanted to pat Anna, but Anna roared as loudly as she could:

'Will you stay where you are, you naughty girl!'

But Kerstin didn't want to stay where she was. She ran straight to Anna and stroked her, even though Anna didn't want her to, and Anna got a face full of shoe polish. Then I laughed as much as Anna did when I got spinach in my eyes.

We didn't know what to do to get rid of shoe polish so we decided to ask Britta. Anna, who was already covered in it, was going to stay there and hold Kerstin tight beside the fireplace while I ran and asked.

When I told Britta what Kerstin had done, she said:

'A fide pair ob nursery nurses you are!'

Then she blew her nose and turned to face the wall and said she wasn't well and didn't know how you got rid of shoe polish.

During this time Olle had come in from the barn and he went absolutely wild when he caught sight of Kerstin.

'Have you taken leave of your senses?' he shouted. 'Have you painted her black?'

We tried to explain to him that it wasn't our fault, but Olle was angry and said it ought to be against the law for people like us to become nursery nurses, and in any event we were to find another child to practise on.

But all three of us helped to heat up water in a big pan and then we carried it out to the grass. We led Kerstin there and as she walked across the floor she left sweet little black footprints behind her. We popped her in the pan and scrubbed her really well all the way from top to toe. We washed her hair too, and she got some soap in her eyes. And then she screamed so that she could be heard all over Noisy Village, and Lasse and Bosse came running up and asked if we were killing pigs.

'Nope,' said Olle. 'It's just these two wonderful nursery nurses practising.'

The shoe polish wouldn't quite come off entirely. When we had finished scrubbing and had dried Kerstin, she was an odd grey colour all over her body. But at least she was happy. She ran around on the grass completely naked, shouting 'Lo, lo' and laughing so you could see all the little rice grains in her mouth. And Olle said:

'She's lovely, that girl.'

We thought that probably the grey colour would wear off eventually, so that the pink child underneath would appear again. Getting on for Christmas, Lasse thought.

Afterwards Olle laid Kerstin in her cot. And she didn't make a peep. All she did was stick her thumb in her mouth and fall asleep on the spot.

'That's how you should look after children,' said Olle. Then he went and fed the pigs.

Anna and I sat on the kitchen steps and had a rest.

'Poor Auntie Lisa, having to put up with this every day,' said Anna. 'I think what it said in the newspaper was a lie because it makes no difference at all *how* you talk to little children. Whether you talk nice and gently or you yell at them, they do exactly what they want anyway.'

Then we were quiet for a long time.

'Anna, are you going to be a nursery nurse when you grow up?' I asked.

'Perhaps,' said Anna. But then she looked thoughtful and stared over the top of the barn roof and said:

'Though I don't really know, now . . .'

WE GO CRAYFISHING

Deep in the forest is a lake called Nocken. You can't go swimming in Nocken because there is so much mud on the bottom. But you can catch crayfish there. Oh, so many crayfish there are! Lasse says there is no other lake in the land of Sweden that is stuffed with as many crayfish as Nocken.

Sometimes Anna says to me:

'Ha, ha, North Farm Lake only belongs to me! Poor you, you haven't got a lake!'

But then I say:

'I have got a lake! What's Nocken if it isn't a lake?'

'Ha, ha, well it doesn't only belong to you, because all of us in Noisy Village can use it,' Anna says. 'So it's mine as much as yours. Ha, ha, that means I've got two lakes, I have,' she says.

That makes me angry and I don't play with Anna any more that day. But the following day we agree that it's all the same whose lakes they are, because all of us swim in North Farm Lake and catch crayfish in Nocken. Only those of us who live in Noisy Village are allowed to catch crayfish there, and I think that's a good thing.

You can't start crayfishing until August. The day it starts is nearly as much fun as Christmas Eve, because then all of us Noisy Village children, apart from Kerstin of course, go with Dad and Uncle Nils and Uncle Erik to Nocken. We lay out the crayfish traps in the evening and then we make camps in the forest and sleep there overnight, and then get up very, very early the next morning and inspect the crayfish traps. That's the best thing of all—being allowed to sleep in the forest at night. Nocken is so far away from Noisy Village and getting there is so difficult that it isn't worth going home to sleep for a few hours, says Dad. What a good job it is that Nocken is so far into the forest after all! Otherwise Mum would definitely make us come home and sleep in our beds.

'I'm so afraid the children will catch a cold,' says Mum every single year.

'Oh, rubbish!' Dad says then. He said that this year too. And after he had said it, we left.

You have to walk more than five kilometres through the forest to get to Nocken, and only a narrow little path winds its way there. We had so much to carry, crayfish traps and blankets and backpacks filled with all sorts of things. But there's no point moaning if you get tired, because then dad says that anyone who moans can't join in with the crayfishing or sleep in the forest overnight.

As soon as we reached the lake we ran to see if there was anything left of the camps we had last year. But there were only a few shrivelled juniper bushes and other old branches and things that we cleared out of the way then and there. Britta and Anna and I make our own camp under a big fir tree. The branches hang down almost to the ground. Dad and Uncle Erik chop down juniper bushes for us and we prop them around the fir tree until there is only an opening in one place big enough to crawl in and out of. Then we put a thick layer of fir tree branches on the ground for us to sleep on.

When we had finished we went to look at the boys' camp. They always make theirs in a crack in the rocks which they cover with sticks and branches so that it's like a roof. And then they have fir tree branches to sleep on, of course.

'How nice it would be if only the girls would leave you in peace in your own camp,' Lasse said, when we turned up to have a look.

And then Bosse and Olle also said it would be nice if the girls left them in peace.

'Who cares?' said Britta. 'As it happens we have a much better camp to be in than this pathetic thing.'

Then Lasse and Bosse and Olle laughed and said they felt sorry for us because we didn't know a single thing about making camps. Before we had time to think of a good answer, Uncle Nils called to us and said we had to come and help with the crayfish traps. The crayfish traps are made of net and they have to be repaired every year. There are always big holes here and there and you mustn't have them because then the crayfish crawl out. We sat on some flat rocks down by the lake and mended the crayfish traps with string, and chatted and had lots of fun. The sun was on its way down and it was very beautiful around the lake, and so quiet. When we weren't talking, of course.

'It's a fine lake, is Nocken,' said Dad.

Uncle Erik was busy bailing out the two old rowing boats that we keep at Nocken. There was a lot of water in them. Uncle Nils and Dad were putting the bait in the traps. When everything was ready we rowed out in the boats and laid the traps in the water all along the edge of the lake. We have our special places where we lay the traps every year.

By the time we had rowed round the whole lake and laid the traps it was starting to get dark. And then Anna pinched my arm and said:

'It's *almost* more fun than Christmas Eve!'

I thought so too, because when it got dark Dad lit a fire on the rocks, like he usually does. And we sat around it, all of us, and got out our thermos flasks with hot chocolate and drank, and ate sandwiches with it. The fire shone across the water so that it looked as if the lake was burning as well. It was so dark in the forest around us, and completely silent. And Lasse said:

'I can hear the trolls tiptoeing around in there among the trees.'

Anna and I got very scared. Although Anna said: 'Huh, there aren't any trolls.'

But we couldn't help listening anyway, just in case we did hear trolls tiptoeing about in the darkness. But we didn't hear anything, and we told Lasse so.

'Nope, that's because their feet are so hairy,' said Lasse. 'They creep around very quietly and they stand behind the trees, watching us.'

'Ooh, of course they don't,' I said, and I moved a little closer to Anna.

'Oh yes they do,' said Lasse. 'The entire forest is full of trolls' eyes, staring at us right now. But they don't dare come here because they are afraid of fire.'

Then Dad said that Lasse shouldn't sit there filling the little girls' heads with things that aren't true. And then Dad put some more branches on the fire and it flared up and lit everything up so beautifully. I don't think there are trolls, but just to be on the safe side I crept up onto Dad's lap, and then Anna went and sat on Uncle Erik's lap. And Uncle Erik whistled for us. He's very good at whistling, is Uncle Erik. He can whistle like a bird if he wants to.

I thought that if there really were trolls in the forest, they would be wondering why we were sitting around a fire listening to Uncle Erik whistling when it was the middle of the night, practically.

They told stories too, Uncle Nils and Dad and Uncle Erik. And we laughed, because they were such funny stories. Lasse and Bosse and Olle took their torches and went down to the water's edge to look for crayfish. They found twenty-three and put them in a tin bucket. And Lasse said to Bosse and Olle:

'If the girls are nice and behave like proper people, we can invite them to a crayfish party tomorrow evening.'

'Yes, but that depends of course on how they behave,' said Bosse.

'It would have to be very good behaviour, in that case,' said Olle.

When the fire had almost gone out Uncle Erik said it was time to go to sleep. The dads didn't have their own camp, so they rolled themselves in blankets and stayed beside the fire. But Britta and Anna and I crawled in under our lovely tree and we rolled ourselves in blankets, too, and were thinking of going to sleep when we heard something tiptoeing outside. And I shouted out:

'Who is it?'

'A troll,' said Lasse, as scarily as he could. We peered out of the opening in the fir tree branches, and there outside stood the boys, shining their torches and saying they wanted to see our camp. They came crawling in, one at a time, and there was room for all of us, even though we were squashed. The boys said it was a pretty good camp we had, although not as good as theirs, of course. Then they crawled out again, and Lasse said:

'A pretty decent camp, that's what it is. But it's not troll-proof!'

Then the boys left, and we tried to sleep. At first we chatted a bit, but it sounds so odd when you lie in the forest and talk at night. It sounds as if someone is standing outside in the dark, listening.

I think Anna and Britta fell asleep long before me. I lay awake for such a long time, listening to the sighing in the forest. It only sighed a little. And small waves came and lapped at the shore ever so gently. It was very strange—all of a sudden I didn't know if I was sad or happy. I lay there and tried to feel if I was sad or happy, but it didn't work. Perhaps you go a bit odd, sleeping in the forest.

Dad came and woke us when it was four in the morning. And then I was only happy, even though I was as cold as a block of ice. But the sun was shining and we crawled out of our camp and slapped our arms around our bodies and jumped up and down and were given hot chocolate by Dad. There was some mist over the lake but it soon disappeared. Dad and Lasse and Bosse and I took one boat, and Uncle Erik and Uncle Nils and Olle and Britta and Anna took the other, and we rowed out to collect the crayfish traps.

I feel sorry for anyone who has never rowed out on a lake and collected crayfish traps at four in the morning.

Nearly every trap was full of crayfish. Lasse and Bosse are brave enough to take hold of the crayfish any way they can, but not me. Bosse picked up a crayfish and sat looking at her, then suddenly he dropped her back in the lake again.

'Are you mad?' shouted Lasse. 'What are you doing, sitting there throwing crayfish into the lake?'

'Her eyes looked very sad,' said Bosse.

'Oh, how stupid you are,' said Lasse. 'Now she'll dart about and tell tales to all the other crayfish in the lake, and we won't get any crayfish this year. What did you let her go for?'

'Her eyes looked very sad,' said Bosse again.

But at that moment we met the other boat, and we yelled to Olle and Britta and Anna:

'Have you got many crayfish?'

'The whole boat full, almost,' yelled Olle.

Then we rowed back to our camping place and there we emptied all the crayfish into two big laundry baskets with lids. And we packed up everything we had at the camp and set off home to Noisy Village. There was dew on the grass and there were spiders' webs here and there on the branches, and they shone like diamonds. I was sleepy and hungry, I had wet feet and I was very, very happy, because it was such fun to walk in a long line on the path and have such masses of crayfish to take home. Uncle Erik whistled and sang.

'A *hunter went a'hunting*

Within a glade so green' we sang. All of a sudden Lasse shouted:

'I can see the smoke from Noisy Village now!'

And then we all saw the smoke rising up over the forest. It was smoke from three chimneys, so we knew that they were awake in North Farmhouse, Middle Farmhouse and South Farmhouse. And when we had walked a little bit further we saw the whole of Noisy Village. The sun shone on the window panes and it was so beautiful.

'I feel sorry for people who don't have anywhere to live,' I said to Anna.

'I feel sorry for anyone who doesn't live in Noisy Village,' said Anna.

Grandad was already awake and sitting under the elm tree that grows on the grass in front of North Farmhouse. And when he heard us coming he called:

'Are there any crayfish in Nocken this year?' And then Uncle Erik said that there were so many crayfish that Grandad had probably never seen anything like it. But then Grandad said:

'Heh, heh, heh. Don't you go forgetting the almighty number of crayfish I've hauled up from Nocken in my time.'

We sat on the grass next to Grandad and told him how much fun it had been. Lasse opened the tin box with the boys' own crayfish and let Grandad listen to them. There's a special kind of sound crayfish make when they crawl around each other. Klirr klirr, it sounds like. Grandad laughed happily and said:

'Aha, sounds like crayfish. No mistaking that.'

And then Lasse said:

'Grandad, can we have a crayfish party at yours this evening?'

'Heh, heh, heh, course you can,' said Grandad.

Astrid Lindgren

Astrid Lindgren was born in Vimmerby, Sweden in 1907. In the course of her life she wrote over 40 books for children, and has sold over 145 million copies worldwide. She once commented, 'I write to amuse the child within me, and can only hope that other children may have some fun that way too.'

Many of Astrid Lindgren's stories are based upon her memories of childhood and they are filled with lively and unconventional characters. Perhaps the best known is *Pippi Longstocking*, first published in Sweden in 1945. It was an immediate success, and was published in England in 1954.

Awards for Astrid Lindgren's writing include the prestigious Hans Christian Andersen Award. In 1989 a theme park dedicated to her—*Astrid Lindgren Värld* (Astrid Lindgren World)—was opened in Vimmerby. She died in 2002 at the age of 94.

Read more about Lisa and her friends in

The Children of
Noisy Village

Happy Times in
Noisy Village

Everything's fun with Pippi around!

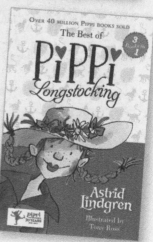